Blackberries in the Dream House

DIANE FRANK

1st WORLD
LIBRARY
Literary Society

AUSTIN • FAIRFIELD • DELHI

Blackberries in the Dream House.
Copyright ©2003 by Diane Frank.

1ST WORLD LIBRARY
PO Box 2211, Fairfield, Iowa 52556
www.1stworldlibrary.com

COVER AND BOOK DESIGN:
Shepley Hansen

COVER ART:
"The Chinese Fishing Party" by François Boucher

JAPANESE CALLIGRAPHY:
"Snow, Moon, Flower" — John Stimson

PHOTOGRAPH:
Anders Hansen

BLACKBERRIES IN THE DREAM HOUSE WEBSITE:
www.dianefrank.net

FIRST EDITION
Library of Congress Catalog Card Number: 9963473
ISBN: 1-887472-68-1

Erotic and metaphysical . . .

"What would happen to us if we were to undertake the discipline of turning our life entirely and self-consciously into a poem? Through Yukiko, who becomes both a contemplative Buddhist and a geisha skilled in the refinements of sensuous pleasure, Diane Frank allows us to live within the soul of a young woman who has undertaken to create a life imagined and expressed as a poem, in every moment, waking and sleeping, making love or meditating. With its power of language, *Blackberries in the Dream House* will seduce many readers into considering whether a prosaic life is the only choice we have."

—Pierre DeLattre
Author of *Walking on Air*
and *Tales of a Dalai Lama*

"Diane Frank's exquisite sensibility manifests throughout in *Blackberries in the Dream House*; it is both erotic and metaphysical. In fact, her great strength is that for her there's no division between the two. The result is this fine lyrical novel."

—Stephen Dunn
Pulitzer Prize Winning Poet

"*Blackberries in the Dream House* gets to you like a caress from the most longed-for and tender of lovers. It turns you on and heals your heart. Diane Frank is a poet goddess whose exquisite incantation will leave you naked in your own sacred house of dreams."

—Alan James Mayer
Talk Show Host,
Radio Producer

"Reading *Blackberries in the Dream House* is like reading one continuous prose poem. You step into a floating world of piercing beauty, wild magic, and earth-shaking emotions. For days I walked around dazed, lost in the dream."

—Caree Connet
Author of *Searching for Entrance*

"'When you remove everything that is not necessary, something glows underneath.' This novel glows with Diane Frank's poetic and visionary wisdom, through an erotic journey illuminating universal cycles of birth, death and rebirth. After having immersed yourself in the sacred lives of Yukiko, a geisha, and the young monk, Kenji, in an older, artistically flowering Japan, you might feel, as I did, along with Yukiko, 'My feet are slices of melon, birds curling over rocks. Where have they taken me now?'"

—Diane Averill
Author of *Beautiful Obstacles*

"*Blackberries in the Dream House* is a passionate novel written by a poet. It is told using deeply saturated images by a woman who lives with vibrating intensity. Frank has a keen eye for the terror and majesty of falling in love, and a kind heart for the circuitous paths the heart takes to escape."

—Terry Brennan
Reviewer, *The Chicago Reader*

"The novel meets the poem in this lovely book with the most exquisite seamlessness. The beauty of language and image Diane Frank is able to maintain, line after line, seems to flirt with the miraculous."

—Nancy Berg
NEA Award Winning Poet

I want to express my deep appreciation to
Alan James Mayer for his creative inspiration and
guidance, to Izumi Nakamura and Paul Shimura for
their help with the Japanese, to Rodney Charles at
1st World Library for understanding my novel and
deciding to publish it, and to Penny Minkler,
Caree Connet, and Suzanne Niedermeyer for
their skill and care in proofreading.

TABLE OF CONTENTS

"Lovers don't meet along
the road somewhere.
They're in each other
all along."
—*Rumi*

Kyoto

One hundred and fifty years ago ...

1

CHILD OF THE SNOW

lackberry soap, wooden buckets, rivulets of steaming water over your shoulders in waterfalls, cascading over the seashell curves of the muscles in your arms. Then back into the steam of the blue-tiled tub in the bath house. I do this with my hands.

You are a Zen Buddhist monk and I am your almond Aphrodite. The monks in the temple call you Kenji, but I call you Lotus Sun.

My name is Yukiko, "Child of the Snow." My parents named me this because I was born in February on the night of the full moon, while the sky was white and full of crystals. I am twenty-one years old, and I am a geisha in Kyoto. I live in Pontocho.

In our tradition we know that before you are born, you meet with the Snow Angels to learn about your path on the jade and sapphire jewel the humans call Earth. The Snow Angels told me the last seven times I traveled to this lovely oasis flying through space, I was a monk or a priestess in the temple. They brought me to different places each time I slid down the Earth Tunnel, and wherever I went, I learned to sing the language of God. There are different melodies around the Flying Jewel, but they all blend together on their way back home.

"This time," the angels told me, "you will go to the land of Japan and be a geisha. You will learn music, poetry, dancing, gentle conversation, and the art of love. You have served well as a priestess, but there is a song in your blood that wants to know other things. It is time now."

I bowed my head and started drifting down on the snow clouds to my mother's home, where her belly was curved like a moon cake. For a while I hovered around her like a firefly. Then I lived inside her for seven moons, until she pushed me out. It's hard and painful to be born, and as you crawl down the Snake Tunnel, you forget everything.

2

THE SEVENTH
DAUGHTER

 am seven years old, the seventh daughter of Miyuki and Unkai. Miyuki means "beautiful snow" and Unkai means "sea of clouds." My sisters are Satomi, "beautiful country"; Satsuki, "May"; Mika, "beautiful fragrance"; Haruna, "ripe spring blossom"; Ogin, "silver beauty"; and Chiyoko, "one thousand generations." My parents have money enough for only three of our dowries, so the rest of us will be geishas. All of our neighbors told my parents to stop making girls after three, but they could not stop loving each other.

When I am twelve years old, I go to the Nadeshiko Geisha House in Pontocho. For the next five years, I will be trained as a maiko in the geisha arts. Nadeshiko is a beautiful flower, like a shy young woman. I live in the teahouse now in a simple room with a tatami mat, a lantern, and a screen with the sumi-e ink tones of winter trees on snow mountains. I will learn to write poetry and I will learn to dance. First with the other girls, and then for the gentle-men who come to the teahouse.

I don't want to play the shamisen because everyone does that, so I learn to play the koto and the shakuhachi flute. Even though I am a girl, I have my own mind.

When I get older, I will learn the art of gentle conversa-tion and the art of love. The older women will teach me. But not until a few years after my first river of peach blossoms falls.

3

FORBIDDEN
DREAMS

 ow I am twenty-one years old. I spend my evenings dancing with painted fans for the gentlemen who eat sushi in the tea-house. Sometimes I serve them saki, and sometimes I sing for them behind the shoji screens.

My favorite visitor is only a few years older than I am. Eitaro has beautiful eyes and strong, wide muscles in his arms and legs. He tells me my breasts are rosebuds and the secret place between my legs is as sweet as a persimmon. But I am the soft blue butterfly he will never let himself catch. He comes from a higher level of society, and marriage with a geisha is forbidden. It causes us pain, but I put my feelings into the shakuhachi tunes I play for him after we make love.

As a geisha I have been trained not to fall in love with my clients. We engage them deeply in art and joyful conversation, but inside we keep a cool detachment. Like shaved ice. Okasan, the Mother of our geisha house, says that women of the flower and willow world keep their feelings inside. We serve men, and that is the source of our power. But in matters of love, I am a woman with my own ways. Eitaro is my first love, my initiation into the mystery of the body. This lake is hot, and I have fallen in over my head.

In the beginning he only came here one or two times a week, but now it is much more often. He waits for me until the end of the evening and sleeps with me every night. I love his wide muscles, his open face, his cheekbones, the warmth of his eyes, and the pleasure in his hands. I love his deep, musical voice. When I have a day without other obligations, we go hiking in the mountains, and he sings to me. I have never been so happy.

We have secret names for one another. He calls me his wild orchid, his sweet persimmon. Week after week he tells me I am the wild and lovely woman he has wanted since the beginning of time. We dream about our future and talk about our life together.

We want to have two children, and he tells me they will be beautiful. He says we will have a girl with almond eyes and my dancer's body, and a boy with wide muscles and his voice. But his parents don't approve, and he is still their son. They have arranged a marriage for him with a kimono merchant's daughter, and they will cut off his inheritance if he doesn't obey.

Eitaro tells me not to worry about the future, but it troubles me. I think we should leave Japan on a boat and cross the Great Ocean. I've heard stories from silk merchants of a new land and a new life where people are more free. But when I mention this to Eitaro, he doesn't want to talk about it. He says we don't need to worry about that now.

4

WHERE MY
BREATHING WHISPERS

itaro wraps me in yellow silk during a thunderstorm. He wakes me up from a dream of cicadas flying away from the feet of a Kabuki dancer. He reaches for me through the song of a wooden flute weaving through branches of rhododendron trees blooming in the rain.

Eitaro loves me like rain, like jasmine petals, like thunder. His scent is sweeter than jasmine, wild like the musk of a brown deer. I love to inhale his skin between the petals of my dreams and in the morning. He loves me like mist in the early morning, scattering dew in a garden of chrysanthemums. I wonder if these are seeds that will grow children.

Sometimes Eitaro frightens me with his intensity. He storms into my house after midnight and ties my wrists with black silk ribbons. He doesn't smile. He won't let me say anything until I am filled with his rain. Until my petals open to him completely. But when he sees the storm of love in

my eyes, he is the one who is frightened. I don't completely understand this.

Eitaro loves me from underneath my muscles, from the
secret place where my breathing whispers. He plays my
body like a master musician on a shakuhachi flute — a winding, weaving melody. His fingers run like deer through the
forest of my body, touch me like summer rain, chrysanthemums blooming in a stone garden. He feels my energy rise,
fill, become the full moon, ripple and scatter like silver fish
in a koi pond. He is an artist of a lover, and he never stops
until the moon is overflowing.

I dance for him in the teahouse and later in the dark,
inside a steam of jasmine flowers. He holds me in the air,
and his mouth is a lake full of kisses, but there are things
that he won't talk about. If I ask him why, he puts his fingers to my mouth. He wants me to be happy, and sometimes
this requires silence.

In my dreams I gather stones from the north, from a blue
lake in the mountains. One of the stones is rose pink, one
is silver. The stones are on my altar now. I wait for answers,
but the stones are silent. The hummingbirds tell me the light
will return at the time of the winter solstice. Then the
stones speak, but in a cryptic language: "Earth brings memory. Ocean brings renewal."

I think Eitaro is someone I could dream with for the rest
of my life. But maybe it's dangerous to think this way. A
dream inside of a stone. He is wealthy, and I am a geisha.

5

HEART FULL
OF SNOW

y love for Eitaro is strong, but I am not happy, even when the sun shines like a bright peach through the slats in my bamboo window. He doesn't come as often anymore, and when I talk about our children, he puts his fingers to my mouth. Sometimes I want to bite them.

My passion for Eitaro is strong as the mountain to the north. My heart knows the shape of every mountain trail we have walked upon. My fingers have memorized the shape of every muscle in his back. But when he leaves, the mountain is covered with snow, and I am buried below a waterfall. My heart sings during our love nights in the teahouse, but on the inside, the whole thing feels impossible. My sister Chiyoko reminds me geishas should never fall in love with their clients — it's too dangerous. But it's too late for that. The first time Eitaro touched me, I was gone.

Now I wait for Eitaro at night in the humid air under

the waving paper lanterns of the teahouse, but more often than not, he doesn't come. I look for him in the crowds of lovers walking so close on the paths by the Kamo River, but he isn't there.

Sometimes on Tuesdays, the monks from the Buddhist temple across the river come to teach us about the ways of our ancestors. We laugh about this behind our fingers. Hiroko says they are really coming to stare at our ankles and glance at the half moon curves of our breasts inside the silk of our kimonos. But I think I will go this time because my heart is full of snow. I have no peace.

6

A SWEET AND SILENT MUSIC

enji is seven years older than I am. His parents brought him to the Zen temple when he was five years old, and he has lived with the monks for more years now than I have walked on the Emerald Jewel. He has been sheltered from the ways of the world since the time he was a young boy. The monks say he is bright with spiritual knowledge. At first he did not want to walk the path to our teahouse in Pontocho, but the Roshi insisted that he was the right one to go.

It isn't the Buddhist way to say that the life of a geisha is wrong, but Kenji says there is more to life than this. The last time we met, he told me, "There is a silver star in your heart that you still need to find. If you listen, you will find that the silver plays a sweet and silent music." He says that my heart has a fragrance sweeter than persimmons, and it will float into my nostrils when I am in my room alone. He has given me a branch of peach blossoms for my room and

11

a statue of Buddha he carved out of cherry wood as part of his spiritual practice. He has also given me a sacred sound to use for meditation.

Every Tuesday he comes to the garden in back of the tea-house to speak to us, and I stare deeply into the lotus sunlight of his eyes. Kenji is tall for a Japanese man. If I stood close to him, my head could nest like a songbird on his chest. His voice is soft and deep, and something about the way he speaks fills me with a quiet peace.

Like all the monks, Kenji's head is shaved, but he has a handsome face. His eyes are warm, and his cheekbones are high and strong. His hands are long and aristocratic. If I let myself daydream, I can almost hear music in his hands, but this is forbidden. Instead I ask him questions about the deeper meaning of life, and at night when my clients leave, I think about the answers. It is a different kind of music than I have heard before, but the tune is sweet.

I am beginning to have memories of life in a different time, but they come in iridescent ripples I can only see behind shadows. I remember bringing peaches to a temple by a river in a round copper bowl. Behind the river I see date palms and sand. I remember chanting in front of an altar in a language I can't remember clearly now. I am wrapped in robes of white.

Eitaro is gone now. He says I am the cherry blossom he can't bring into his home, the sweet moon that in fourteen days has to become new again. He has obeyed the will of his family. In the spring he will marry someone else. My heart has snapped like a thin twig of bamboo, but I have become the wind that pushes through the branches. I am glowing like an indigo butterfly wing a monk finds in the open palm of Buddha.

7

A WILD
SACRED DANCE

Kenji wants to visit me alone. He says he will come on Thursday. I have some fear about this, but he says that I am wise beyond my years and he wants to help the silver star in my heart grow brighter. He wants to give me a book with wisdom about spiritual illumination. He says I have a light that is deeper and brighter than most people he has met, and maybe I want to ask him some questions that I am shy to speak in front of my friends. Since I was a small child, I have always had dreams that later come true. Maybe I will tell him about this.

I think Kenji has questions he would like to ask me too. No one has told me this, but the hummingbirds flying over the koi pond have whispered in my ear. From the time I was very young, I have known things that nobody tells me.

Now I see him walking through the garden on the path beside the persimmon trees. He comes to my door, which

13

is open, and I offer him a seat on a silk pillow beside the lilies I have arranged for him on the tatami mat. I bring him bancha tea and tangerines on a lacquer tray, black and purple with yamato-e irises.

I am afraid to look into his eyes as we sit with the woody steam of the tea between us. This makes him laugh in a voice that reminds me of the sparkle of water over stones in a waterfall, but my life is so different from his. If I open the petals of my face, maybe he will see too deeply. Kenji ignores my hesitation. We sit for a while in silence. Then he takes rice paper out of his shoulder bag, mixes his ink, and brushes calligraphic shapes into the emptiness.

I watch his hands as he shows me how. They have the innocence of a young boy who has never been touched by a woman, and the wisdom of the roots of a tree that has lived for a hundred years. I watch his long, thin fingers as the sepia ink washes over the paper in mysterious lines that ripple like a koi pond. Along the edge of the page, he paints a haiku that just flew into his ear from out of nowhere. It celebrates the first morning light through a spray of cherry blossoms, but I know the poem is about me.

Now it is my turn. My hands are moving almost by themselves, in a way I can't explain or understand. The sepia ink is a wild sacred dance, something I have felt before but only in my body. Now I feel it in my heart and my hands. I am swimming in a rice harvest. The ink is a ripple of leaves, a flow of plum branches waving across the moon, a wild geometry in graded shades of moonlight.

Kenji says that calligraphy is a spiritual practice, like archery, or the simple arrangement of chrysanthemums in a vase. When you remove everything that is not necessary, something glows underneath. He tells me I am like that too, and in time I will see. Then he gives me a book of the teachings of the Buddha and says good-bye. He says that we can

14

all become Buddhas, and that he will return in a week.

It is almost evening — the sun is a tangerine low in the sky. I press my face against the slatted screen and follow him with my eyes as he walks on the winding stone path through the garden. Then he disappears behind a branch of cherry blossoms.

8

A
GENTLE ART

t is Thursday again, and Kenji walks through my open door. We have been painting together for three months now, in sumi-e ink tones. The bamboo walls around the silent place where I dream are filled with wild calligraphic shapes, both his and mine. But something in his eyes is different today.

Kenji gazes at me before he speaks — it is a long, full silence. "I have been guiding you to the inner secrets of Zen calligraphy for more than three moons now."

"While the moon has risen, swelled, and disappeared like the belly of my mother birthing girls. While dragonflies skim the upper edge of the koi pond." I answer him with my eyes instead of my fingers.

"You have done well." He continues to speak as his eyes dance over the sumi-e onions, plum branches, and cicada moon brushed paintings around the room. "Now there is a gentle art that you know better than I do, and it is time for you to begin to teach me."

Kenji says he wants to visit me after midnight. I tell him it is forbidden, but he is strong in his desire. He has never been touched by a woman's hands, and he wants to know this mystery. I am frightened, but I don't say anything. I feel like I am falling into the woven patterns of the tatami mat under our feet.

He sees my fear, but still he is smiling. "Since the morning of my sixth birthday, I have lived with the monks in Oshidoridera across the river from your geisha home. Except for my mother when I was very young, I have never been touched by a woman's hands. I want you to give me a bath."

I remind him of his vows, but he will not be dissuaded. He is laughing as he falls into the night pools of my eyes.

"I will not break my vows, but I need to know this mystery. I will come to you tonight after the temple bells ring for the last time."

9

HOUSE
OF DREAMS

 leave my door open, and when the moon is above the trees, I hear the soft music of his steps. He walks through the door in silence, and in silence I take his hand. As I lead him across the stones to the bath house, our arms are patterned in moonlight through jasmine leaves.

I continue to lead him in silence across the courtyard and around the persimmon garden. The moonlight is flooding its pearls through the open spaces between the leaves.

Now we walk up the steps to the bath house, and I open the door to the blue tiled room he dreamed about three nights ago. Slowly I light seven candles in an ascending arc. I turn then in my kimono, catch the half moons of his eyes with my own. He is in my world now as I say slowly, softly, "Welcome to the House of Dreams."

Kenji starts to untie his robe, but I stop him with a soft touch of my fingers. I tell him, "This is mine to do." Slowly,

19

softly, I remove his robe like the petals of a persimmon and lay them on the painted screen.

I am his almond Aphrodite as he follows me into the water. He is a man and a child at the same time. Now he is shoulder high in lotus water. His face looks like a Buddha surrounded by a halo of steam in front of the blue tile walls of the sky. And tonight the sky is an expanding horizon.

Slowly, I circle a bar of blackberry soap into lather in my hands. The dream house water is warm as a human being can stand, but I see him shiver. I haven't touched him yet, but twenty-eight years of anticipation ripple up his spine.

I am never in a hurry. My hands are hummingbirds hovering, dancing towards him in the steam, softly flying home. With soapy hands I trace the wings of a butterfly over his heart and close my eyes. Yes, this is the place to start. When I touch him, I see his light flow into mine. He closes his eyes and he feels my light flow back. Then I expand the light through his body.

Now I follow the light with my hands. My hands are exploring the muscles, the lines, the geography of his body. I trace his lips with my fingers. Then I brush them across his cheeks and his eyes. I circle his shoulders and run my hands along the landscape of his arms. Then I massage his legs. His muscles are deeply tanned and stronger than I expected on a monk's body. Before this moment I didn't know how much of a man I would find. Kenji laughs at my surprise and my delight.

I slide behind him, and my fingers get lost in the music of his back. This is a new country, and I want to memorize everything. Kenji is breathing the language of my fingers. Breathing deeply. His smile is like a Buddha, but at the same time he is a man. This is a mystery.

As I cup the water over his shoulders with my hands, I see the shape of another bath house in the steam. It is almost

like I am dreaming, but I am not. The bath house is made
of sandy stone in a country where women give birth to their
babies in a river with the name of a snake.

I am almost lost in that river, but the steam brings me
back to the blue tiled room in Kyoto where we are shoulder
high in hot water. Candles light the walls in a flood of
amber petals. Kenji is walking towards the shore of a land
where he has never been. He's swimming toward a new horizon.

My long black hair floats around me in the water. I lean
back and look into his eyes. He laughs before he speaks and
I can almost breathe his delight. "I never understood about
heaven from reading the sacred texts, but it's so clear now,
so easy. The way to know heaven on earth is in the body.
Your body is the most beautiful and sacred jewel in the
world."

We are both shoulder high in steaming water. His hands
have observed strict rules for many years, and now they want
to know everything. They are explorers on a wild coast of
new water. He reaches out and slowly touches my face, my
hands, my arms, my shoulders, my breasts. I close my eyes
and shiver inside the steam. He touches so carefully, so completely. I feel like sculpture under his hands.

Now he is standing in front of me on the wood, wearing
only the robes of his ochre-tinted skin, lit by candles. He is
my path to God, and he is kneeling before me now, an unexpected gift after midnight, a quiet saint hidden inside a sculpture of long muscles. I trace the shape of his arms with the
soft fur of willows until every continent of his body is an
island lit by sparks. Then I begin to use my hands.

Slowly I anoint him with geranium oil. I circle the seven
sacred lotuses of his body with my fingers. Then I spread
oil wherever my fingers want to go. This is a river to heav-
en, and I am the hands of the waterfall. He is the sun on

21

the water as it sprays over unexpected rocks. We are swimming in secret passageways through a mystery he has never known. Candles burn as we forget about time.

We swim in a blue tiled universe without edges until the birds of dawn ring their sacred bells in the early light. As I clothe him in the petals of his monk's robe, he kisses the top of my head. Then he leaves quickly.

10

FORBIDDEN MYSTERY

ach time Kenji visits me, I offer him a painting and a poem. I have them waiting on my silk pillow. I have been painting a series of onions in different shades of wash and light. I peel them layer by layer, and paint the skins as they curl around geraniums. I know this is unusual, but I have to paint what is inside me. My poems are images of whatever I dreamed last night.

Kenji tells me how much he loves my paintings and my poems, and I tell him about my dreams. Since I met Kenji, going to sleep at night is like going to school. After I start to dream, I walk through soft light into a mirror, bathe myself in a waterfall, and follow a path of candles to the center of a mountain. I bow there to a group of teachers, some of them women, some of them men. Each night one of them takes my hand and whispers a secret in my ear — something important I need to know — and in the morning I always remember. I write these messages in my poems and paint the landscapes they show me in sepia ink tones.

It's good that I can share this with my friend from the Buddhist temple. The geishas wouldn't understand. Sometimes they chatter to me about painted silk in the market, ivory hairpins, or the fine lines and hard muscles of a handsome client. In March my friend Yayoi will marry a wealthy silk merchant from Nagasaki. He is older, but he adores her. This is a blessing to all of us, but I live in a different world.

My Buddhist friend comes to see me every Thursday just before midnight. He kisses my mouth like a ripe berry, staining his lips. His pleasure is so strong that I feel him shiver. I guide his mouth to the secret part of my body that is like a persimmon. He can hardly contain his joy as the sweet nectar dampens his mouth. His tongue is a silver fish, gliding in and out of a mystical cave of delight. He is ecstatic, full of a secret pleasure.

He wants so much to know the forbidden mystery completely, but this is something I will not permit. If he breaks his vow, he will have to leave the temple and find another home. Sometimes he begs me to teach him the secrets that only I can share. He says it will be a new initiation, more holy than anything he has given me. But there are other ways to please him. Scented oils, my mouth, and my hands.

I anoint Kenji with oil. He is a living sculpture of the hidden face of God. We have become an icon, a deva with four arms, four legs, and a male and female essence breathing. We are the earth, the sky, and all of the constellations. We are the eternal circle of creation and destruction, day and night. I swim in the melody of cat sounds pushing out of his throat. He is a rainbow trout, wildly swimming home.

Kenji doesn't hear what my heart now whispers because he is gone. But I will whisper through the walls, and I'm sure he will hear my voice in the center of his dreams:

"The air is moist, violet, full of rose petals. Even after you leave, you stay inside me.

"We are the sun and moon of the Tao. The darkness and light of the emerald. The crunch and the sweetness of the new pear. The cadence and fall of the cicada's song. I have only known you for the briefest moment, and we have lived together for a thousand years.

"You are a branch of blackberries in the dream house, sweet and ripe. I always sleep inside you."

11

RIVER
OF BIRTH

y sister Mika is expecting her first child, and my parents send for me. My mother brings moon cakes to the geisha house and asks Okasan if I can come with her for a few weeks because my sister needs me at home. Okasan smiles as though she is remembering something from a long time ago. Then she lets me go.

As I follow my mother on the path to our house, I am filled with a quiet joy. I watch her feet and her ankles below the hem of her blue kimono. Her steps are music on the stones, and I follow with my flute. When I was with Eitaro, I wanted his children so much that I cried every month when I saw my river of peach petals fall. At least now, I will share this birth with my sister. I smile again, and my joy is like the music in my flute.

My mother is happy to cook for me again, happy to have her daughters home for the birth. She tells me, "Mika has always been delicate, and you are her favorite sister. She feels calm with you and also strong. A birth is a powerful time for a woman, but it isn't easy. I know the birth will be better with you to help her, and Mika knows it too. That's why she asked for you.

"Even though her belly is round as the full moon, Mika is still a girl in many ways. But she is at the edge of a huge transformation. The womb is a door, and the woman goes through along with the baby. That is the only way the birth can occur.

"At the geisha house, I know you have learned about massage and healing oils. If Mika has any problems, I know you will pull her through. She trusts you, and I do too."

I smile at her, but I am too overwhelmed to say anything. Three nights later, I am sleeping on my futon when my mother comes for me. She is holding a candle. She tells me, "Mika has started labor."

I follow my mother with my oils, my herbs, and my flute. Mika's room is full of candles. They form a circle around her like a cocoon. When the birth pains come, I hold her face and look into her eyes. That's what Okasan told me to do. Mama goes for the midwife, and I remind Mika to breathe.

"You are strong enough to do this. Just breathe when you feel the pains, and soon the baby will come."

She tells me, "I am frightened. I feel like I am splitting in half, and my body is going to break. The pain is too strong for me."

"Keep on breathing, Mika, and the baby will come through. Mama had seven of us, and she is even smaller than you."

Now Mika is screaming. Her screams get higher and higher like a small child who is terrified. I hold her face and breathe my love into her eyes. "You can do it, Mika. There's a river running through you, and your baby is on a tiny boat. Soon the baby will be floating out of you."

The sun comes up, and the birds sing into the morning. A soft breeze blows in through the open window. A dragonfly circles the room, hovers over my sister, and lands on the lacquer vase in the corner. Still the pains continue. Mama brings Mika tea and we hold her up so she can drink. Mama says, "It will be soon, Mika. Just a little bit more."

Birds are singing on plum branches outside the window. The room is filled with a light I can't explain. It feels holy in here — soft and sweet and new. Maybe our ancestors have come down the emerald ladder for the birth. Or maybe there is an invisible helper in the light — maybe one of the angels Kenji told me about. I can't see her but I feel her presence.

I drift away on a blue silk pillow. A few hours later, Mama comes and wakes me. I have been dreaming, flying somewhere else. Maybe it's because I didn't sleep most of the night, or maybe the angel I couldn't see covered me with feathers. Mama takes my hand and leads me into the kitchen. I am still brushing feathers away from my eyes.

Mama looks troubled. I can feel this even before I hear her words. "While you were sleeping, Yukiko, your sister Mika fell asleep too. The birth pains stopped, and the midwife says maybe Mika needs to rest for a while before she pushes the baby out. But now the labor hasn't started again."

"Doesn't the midwife know what to do?"

"She gave Mika some herbs, but the baby is stuck." Mama takes my hands.

I close my eyes for a few minutes. "I don't know how, Mama, but I will find out what to do."

I go back into the birth room and take out my flute. I tell Mika that I will play a song for her first child, and the baby will move again. I know the baby will hear my song.

29

Mika reaches for my hands, and I hold her close to me. "I'm so tired, Yukiko, so tired."

I see this, but I see something else too. Mika is becoming a woman right in front of me. On this birthing bed. I see that she is frightened, but she is also very strong. Stronger than I have seen her before.

"I'm going to play the song now. The music is like a river, and I know the baby will hear. Then your baby will get on the raft and start floating through again."

The music I hear is mysterious — powerful and sweet at the same time. I feel like I am listening to a song from somewhere else. I let the music flow through me, and then I release it through my mouth and my fingers. I know the baby hears — I can almost feel her smiling, but nothing happens.

I put my hands on my sister's belly and close my eyes. I talk to the angel. "I can't see you, but you have to help us. Tell us what to do."

I hear someone whisper. "Your hands are lotuses filled with light, floating on the lake of birth. Keep your hands on the full moon of your sister's belly, one on top, one below. As you feel the baby floating, let your love flow through your hands. Then the labor will start again."

It doesn't take long for the labor to start, and this time Mika welcomes the pain. The midwife hums to herself as she washes Mika's face and shoulders with rose-scented water. The aroma fills the room and the petals float.

Mika is in another world. I can almost feel her open. She doesn't resist the pain the way she did before, but it washes her across a beach where I have never traveled. I feel her body scraping on the sand and the shells. I feel her tumbling underwater. Then I feel her paddle up to the surface to breathe. Okasan told me that Mika would swim to another world, but I didn't know it would be like this.

Mika is roaring like a lion, breathing out of control. I feel

30

like we are all being born. The midwife massages her lower back, where the baby is pushing against her spine, while I massage her shoulders and her hands. Mika is wild like a goddess in the middle of a flood she can't control. The birth pains are stronger and quicker now.

Then, as suddenly as they started, the birth pains stop again. The midwife tells us to let Mika rest for a while. She feeds her miso soup with some onion, herbs and squash. She says this will give Mika the energy to start the birth again. I want to put my hands on her belly again, but the midwife says no.

Now I feel confused and tired. I haven't slept much for two days, and my legs feel like they are filled with sand. Maybe it's sand from the ocean of birth, or maybe from somewhere else. I sit down on a pillow and lean my head against the wall. I can hardly sit up. I've reached a point where I'm way beyond what I know.

Mika starts her labor again, but this time it starts and stops. It isn't the wild flood we saw before.

The moon is pulling up again, and I am filled with old memories — I don't know from where. Suddenly, I am frightened. I don't want my sister to die. I have to see this child. Eitaro is married, Kenji is a monk, and I may never have a child of my own. I am covered by a flood of dark water.

Mika is asleep again, and I run into the kitchen. We've been inside the birth for two nights and two days. Soon the moon will be high above the trees. Mama takes me to her futon and tells me to sleep. She covers me with a red silk quilt she made before I was born, and I sleep until the moon is full in the sky. Then I go back into the kitchen.

Now all of my sisters have come home. Mama tells us to eat so we will be strong enough to help our sister. She will need our help at the end. Mika's labor starts and stops, but it isn't strong enough for the river of birth to push out the baby.

31

I take the midwife's hands. I tell her I am frightened and I ask her what is wrong.

She is patient with me, as she is with my sister and the baby. She tells me, "Some babies take a long time before they decide to be born. They are still hearing the music from the other world. Maybe the light of this world is still too bright for this baby."

I see a wisdom in her eyes, but I am in a panic now. It is a combination of what I don't know and too little sleep. I reach for my flute. If I play the song that sounds like a river, maybe the baby will hear and decide to float out to us again.

I want to put my hands on Mika's belly and tell our baby that this world is beautiful too. This world is also filled with sweet and mysterious music. And a family — we're all waiting to meet you. If I put my hands on Mika's belly, somehow I'll find a way to let the baby hear this through my hands.

I put my flute to my lips, but the midwife stops my hands. I can see from her eyes that she can read my mind. "Mika has to rest," she says. "She has to get stronger."

"What is wrong with my sister?" I am pleading now.

"Mika is still resisting. The pain is going to get much stronger, and something in Mika knows. She's fighting it instead of letting go. We can't help her anymore. She just has to open up and do it.

"To have a baby, you have to lose control. You have to split open. You have to let the pain wash through you in a flood and find the ecstasy. That's when the baby comes."

"But I want to help. I have to help. I'm her sister."

The midwife sighs and continues to speak softly. "Mika is still holding on to the stones at the side of the water. She's still holding on to the branches and the bark. Go to your sister and tell her to open her hands. Tell her to trust the water. She almost did it before, but then she stopped.

"Hold her face and breathe with her. Pour your love into her eyes, and then help her to get wild. Spin her into the wind. Follow her into the water. To have a baby, you have to lose control. You have to go belly first into the water, over your head, into the wildest wave you've ever known."

Right now, I don't know whom to trust. I know the woman in front of me is wise, but we have been in the birth for three nights and two days now. It doesn't feel right to me. This is all good philosophy, but her herbs aren't working. I feel she is at the end of what she knows.

The midwife sees me drifting into the dark again, but she pulls me back with her words. "It's going to be all right, Yukiko. Sometimes you have to trust what you don't know."

I walk into the birth room. Mika is having pains again, but still not like before. I start to speak, but she puts her fingers to my mouth. She is half out of her mind, and she needs me to be silent now. So I sit with her until the birds sing into the morning. A dark cloud covers the sun, and it begins to rain.

Mika is caught between two worlds, and I am swimming with her. I'm trying to keep myself above the water. I close my eyes, and then I hear a voice soft as silk, sharp as crystal, singing out of a cloud. I hear a whisper, "Go to Okasan. She will tell you what you need to do."

I put on my sandals, and I am running down the slate path in the rain. Running over the slick wet stones to the teahouse. Okasan has taught me many secrets, but now I need more.

Okasan opens the door to the teahouse and folds me in her arms. She says, "I've been expecting you. I dreamed about you last night. I know there's trouble in your house. I'm ready — I'm going with you." She puts some herbs and oils into a furoshiki, folds the cloth, and we walk into the rain. We listen to the rain under the same umbrella.

"I will tell you a few secrets while we are walking. Your sister is in transition now, between the worlds, and she will be having the baby soon. I know it's confusing to you because you have never had a child, but right now you have to trust me. I know there is nothing to worry about."

"But how do you know?"

"There are things you know from the center of your body. I had two daughters long before you met me, so I know about birth. Also, I was midwife for many women in the geisha house. I know the stages of birth, and the signs.

"Your sister has been very inward, like she's in another world. Yes?"

"It's like she's in a dream house, and I don't know how to find her anymore."

"That's a good sign. And then you try to help her, and she pushes you away?"

"How did you know? She snapped at me, like a turtle."

"All of this is good. And when you dreamed, you didn't see any gray feathers or red stones?"

"No, the feathers were white and blue."

"Then everything is fine."

"How can a birth that takes three days be fine?"

"It's unusual, but sometimes it happens that way. I'll tell you another secret about birth. There is always a time of confusion. Every woman thinks she can't do it right at the point when she's almost done it. You walk into the dark and you think you're lost until you walk through.

"Now listen to me. When you go back into the birth room, trust your sister. Trust the baby too. Tell her, 'You're doing fine. You're almost there. Just keep breathing with me. Just a few more contractions and you'll be pushing. Then the baby will come through.' And just keep loving her. She'll feel your love and it will make her strong."

Now we're in front of my family house, but Okasan doesn't

34

let me open the door. She says, "There's one more thing you need to know," and she whispers it in my ear. Then we go inside.

All of my sisters are in the birth room now. They are holding candles and chanting the songs the nuns from the temple taught us when we were children. Something about being in this room feels sacred. It's like being inside a cocoon. I bow to my sisters and then I walk inside the circle of light with Okasan.

I am ready to swim again, so I put my feet in the water. Okasan lifts my sister's head and gives her an herb that I have never seen before. "Drink... drink...," she says. When Mika finishes, Okasan takes her hands and pushes hard on two shiatsu points. Then she smiles at me.

I put my hands on the full moon of my sister's belly, and Mika begins to open again. But she is afraid, and her voice is high with pain. The pain is stronger than it was before.

I hold her face and whisper, "There is something Okasan told me — a secret I will tell you. When you feel yourself pull open inside, there are two different rivers. One of them takes you to pain, and the other takes you to joy. Both rivers are there at the same time, and they flow together, side by side. For three days and three nights, you have been floating in the wrong river, and that is why you are feeling pain. Step out of that river now. I will massage your feet while you are resting, and this will send energy through your body. When you feel yourself pull open again, step this time into the river of joy. You will still feel the pain, but it won't control you anymore because the joy is deeper. It's a wild river, but you will float free this time."

I put my hands on her belly again. She is breaking open, but now it's a different sound. Music that I have never heard before. A wild and rushing river. Mika is a goddess out of control becoming a woman right before my eyes.

Mika is groaning, grunting, pushing, wild. She's rain. She's thunder. She's an open sea. Now we see the top of the baby's head between her legs. Then she pushes the baby out in a flood of rushing water.

Our baby is a girl, and her eyes are wide open. I have never seen anyone so beautiful. Gently, Okasan puts the baby on Mika's belly. Her new skin is so soft, her tiny eyes wide and open to her mother's face.

Okasan speaks to me now. "This is the way a baby bonds with her mother and learns to trust the world. Face to face." As we watch, her tiny mouth finds her mother's breast.

I think about Kenji before I fall asleep in my mother's bed. It will be my first easy sleep in three days. I know he will ask me what I have learned, and I'm too tired to think about it now. Too tired and too happy.

I float into the waters of sleep between the worlds. It's calm water now — all of Mika's pain is only a memory. My pain is only a memory too. I watch myself fill with light. Then I hear my own voice speaking to me.

"Loving is like a birth. We're all born in water. We swim for nine months, and then we come out in a flood.

"All of life is birth. You have to live moment to moment. And the most important things you can't control. You just have to let them emerge in their own time and their own way, like a baby."

12

ON DRAGONFLY WINGS

I haven't seen Kenji for weeks because I have been taking care of my sister, but he's coming again on Thursday. I have a pile of dreams in my basket, painted on rice paper in sumi-e ink tones. The Birth Angel told me to show the shape of this paint to Kenji.

But maybe they aren't dreams at all. Maybe they are windows that open to windows in a different place and time. Maybe they are doorways to parallel universes that touch each other's edges and breathe simultaneously. Perhaps they are keyholes that open to a body that lives inside my body — a body that can fold itself like an origami crane and then open somewhere else.

My dreams are crystals of transformation that open to knowledge I couldn't see or feel or touch in my daylight body. A path of stone lanterns. I float in the crystal body of sleep — the spark in the shield around the light that pulls me through space and time on a journey that always arrives home, even if I don't know where home is right now.

I don't experience time the way other people do. That much is getting clear. Often I feel I am several places at the same time — living simultaneously in parallel universes and parallel lives. But it's not the kind of thing I can talk about to most people I see. Especially the people who come here.

The men who visit the teahouse like to talk to me because they never know what I am going to say. Sometimes I bring a basket with rice paper and different shades of ink. I let the conversation get wild and then, when we're really at the edge, I paint the shape of the conversation. Or maybe I'll paint something totally unexpected and tell whomever I'm talking with to hang the painting over his bed before he goes to sleep. I hope he will enjoy getting painted in his dreams.

Sometimes I pull out my shakuhachi flute and finish the conversation in music. Then whomever I'm talking to has to wait until I'm through. I'm never in a hurry.

I sign my paintings in calligraphy, "Yukiko, Child of the Snow," and then I write a few lines of a poem. Maybe more than a few. I never plan it in advance — I just write what I feel. Maybe I'll be famous one day, after I am dead. The men can take my paintings to their wives and tell them, "I stopped on the way home to see a famous artist and poet," instead of, "I stopped on the way home to see the geishas."

I don't know how to explain this, but I feel more powerful since my sister's birth. Also, there's something stronger in my hands. It's almost as though I am living in a different world, even though the shape of everything on the outside is still the same. Or almost the same. On the inside everything is changed.

I want to give Kenji a dream tonight. Maybe I'll tell him in words or maybe in paint. My words will fly to him on dragonfly wings and whisper. They will float like hummingbirds hovering on the path to the Buddhist temple where he sleeps and fly inside his ear. They will sing inside the drops of moisture hanging in the late night air, and he will hear them in his dreams.

Kenji, listen, I'm speaking to you now: "I am the wild lake that ripples through your heart and the dragonfly that rests on your eyelids. I am the artist who paints you while you sleep. Tonight you will have a dream that will change the shape of the crystal through which you see everything."

13

A LADDER
OF FEATHERS

egumi died suddenly on Saturday. She was on the lake in a small wooden boat with her lover in a thunderstorm, and the boat was hit by lightning. I'm told she disintegrated instantly. She ignited, dissolved, and then became a cloud. She became invisible in less than an instant. Megumi was only twenty-two years old. I think if a woman has to die so young, it should be like this. In a thunderstorm. Dripping with love. On rippling water.

All morning the Buddhist monks at Oshidoridera have been chanting the sacred rites for the departed, to help her on her journey. As a child I sometimes walked in the temple gardens, especially in the spring, but I have never been inside. I have always wondered about the temple and how it would feel to be inside. Megumi's family went through the door of light ten years before her, and we are her only family now. We are her sisters, and the monks want us to join them as they chant the sutras of her final prayers.

With candles in our hands, we walk the path by the Kamo River. We bow and offer baskets of cherry blossoms at the Gion Shrine by the Shijo Bridge. I've come this way before, but everything looks different now, even the early afternoon light. We walk up the stone steps to the Buddhist temple and enter the carved wooden door. It is so silent here. So peaceful. We have been weeping, but there is a peace here that goes beyond tears.

The Roshi walks up to us slowly. He is wearing a saffron robe like the one I have come to know so well, but he has a different face. He is older than my father. His face is lined with furrows like the bottom of a river that has seen a life-time of water. Wet years, dry years, floods, and storms. His eyes are like a sky without clouds, but the peace there lets me know that these are eyes that accepted the clouds when they crossed his way. He must have blessed them and then let them go. There is a silence that vibrates through his body. He is a man who is not afraid to die because he has found the right way to live.

Kenji taps a gong suspended from a carved frame with a mallet; then the monks begin chanting. I am swinging between two parallel universes as I follow the swelling cadence of their voices. Part of me feels an immense hole where Megumi used to be. I think about rolling sushi with her on Tuesday. I steam the rice, line nori on the bamboo mat, paint a small line of wasabi on the rice, slice cucumbers, place them over the rice next to small bites of yellow-tail. I think of what I will say to her, and then I imagine her answers. I have already heard her last words, and her voice has to come from inside me now. I am whirling in a vortex that knows she is gone.

Then my foot is suspended on another stone inside a mountain. Kenji has assured me that we don't disappear when we die; we just go somewhere else. If I listen to my heart, I know this is true. Maybe at night I can follow her there. I can fall asleep and then climb a ladder of feathers that will lead me to her voice. When I climb to the top of the ladder, I will find her, and we can finish our conversation. I know there are things she didn't tell me, and now she knows even more.

The Roshi's voice pulls me back to the Buddhist temple. The altar is filled with candles, incense, and flowers. The Roshi is asking if any of us can read the prayer of blessing from her family, and the geishas are pushing me forward. Yesterday, Kenji taught me the chant of the melody, so I take the book from the Roshi's hand. My voice surprises me. It is clear, sweet, and full of something that wasn't there before this moment. I feel my words reaching out to Megumi where she is waiting between the worlds. They are powerful words, and I feel them change her there. Now she is ready for the next part of her journey.

At the end of the ceremony, Kenji hits the gong again, but he is not allowed to speak to me. Not now and not here. The Roshi speaks to us of a peace beyond understanding, and we feel it in his voice and eyes. Then we leave silently while the monks are chanting.

The evening is full of rose-colored light. We weave silk ribbons over the door of the teahouse, and we will keep the door closed for seven days. Two of Megumi's friends are still crying. They ask me to tell them everything I have learned from Kenji about the soul's journey. Where is Megumi sleeping now, and what color is the light? Does the soul have dreams in the other world? Will she have a Snow Angel to guide her? Will she come back? If I speak to her after midnight, will she be able to hear? Before, they used to tease me about my lessons with the monks, but we have all been singed by lightning. We are floating on a river of new awareness. All

43

of us are changed.

Kenji has given me a prayer to chant each night for the next seven weeks. I feel the words enter Megumi as soon as they leave my mouth, and somehow they make me peaceful too. As I sleep, peacock feathers swirl and drift to my face. Then I see the ladder. I climb, pulled by the sweet music of Megumi's voice. She is waiting for me on top of a cloud the color of a rosebud. She pours me jasmine tea.

She says, "I am happy here and I am at peace. I am flying, floating, free, and glad to be done with the lessons of Megumi. When I went into the light, my parents came and took my hands. Then they took me to the house of my ancestors. I was met by a teacher here, a being of light, and everything she says fills me with joy. Please tell my friends that they don't need to worry — I am happy here with the Snow Angels. And let them know that death is a transformation, an open door."

She pours me tea again, and I feel it float through my body out to my fingers. She says, "In the beginning of time, in the holy of holies, we were all filled with light. Now I will give you one of my sparks so part of me will always live inside you."

She puts her hand on my heart and I feel the light enter. She says, "Listen to everything Kenji teaches you. It will all be important when you come back. When the time comes, I will meet you with gardenias in my hands."

Suddenly, I am floating down the ladder. I feel Megumi's light in my heart like a candle that glows rose pink. I float to my tatami mat, and I sleep surrounded with fireflies. They are so bright the swans across the lake can see me glow.

14

THE LOTUS EYES
OF WOMEN

itaro is back at the teahouse today. He has been married for eighteen months, and his face looks different now. His eyes seem smaller, moon slivers too close to the horizon, falling over the edge of space and time. Maybe they are afraid to see as much they did before.

I stay behind the screens, but the geishas tell me his wife is very beautiful. Two of them saw her walking in the market. She wears the kimonos of the upper class, she has servants to cook his food, and her father has taken Eitaro into his business as a son. But I know something is wrong in his house. I can see it in his face. Something about his face has changed.

Eighteen months ago, Okasan told me this was not a marriage of the heart. She said it was a marriage arranged by the families — a liaison of convenience. I can tell from the shadows on his face that his wife is not skilled in the art

45

of love. Their love is not the sweet persimmon he has tasted before. The birds that used to flutter in the light around his face have flown away. He is not happy.

Two weeks ago I painted seven cranes on the screen I hide behind. I am flying with the cranes as they lift their wings to the moon. Eitaro and I haven't spoken yet, but I sit on my heels and watch him. My ears follow the weave of his conversation. Eighteen months with the daughter of the man who sells kimonos, but no children. Her belly stays flat. When Eitaro was my lover, he knew our children would be beautiful.

How I had longed to be with him. I wanted him to weave my kimonos into a dragon kite and soar high above the mountains. I wanted to become the wind, to weave the silk of my pillows into sails on a boat that would carry us east across the sea. I wanted to feel his children growing while my belly swelled purple like an eggplant. I wanted this so much that I wept every month with my peach blossom fall. He wanted all of this too, and I never understood how he could leave me.

Now he is at the teahouse again, drinking the lotus eyes of women he doesn't own, filling himself with forbidden love. He hasn't asked for me yet — maybe he is too ashamed.

15

IN LOVE
WITH A MEMORY

Three weeks later Eitaro is at the teahouse. He fills himself with the sushi Satomi brings on a lacquer tray, sips his sake slowly, and calls my name. This is confusing. He made me so unhappy eighteen months ago, but now I have found another love. Eitaro has never seen my poetry or my painting. He is in love with a memory, but I am not that person anymore.

Okasan asks me to go to him. This is my profession, but not my passion. It is my duty, but not my desire. We speak for a while and then he tells me he wants a bath. Words that crash against my ears. I lead him into the bath house and wash him slowly with my hands, the way I did before, but I don't look at him. My eyes are wild geese, swimming in the blue steam rising from the tiles. My arms are wings that have forgotten how to fly.

Eitaro sees the confusion in my eyes. He watches the geese swimming softly through the haze over the koi pond, follows the monarch butterflies circling into a low hanging cloud. I look up slowly and see that he still loves me — I see it in his eyes. I didn't understand that before. I thought the love wasn't there because he was gone.

For a long time he only looks at me, drinking me in with his eyes. Then he begins to speak softly. "Take your time. You don't have to love me now. I just had to see you. You don't have to be afraid. I will wait until you want me." He kisses my forehead and then he washes my feet. This is something new.

He asks me to sit across from him and lifts my feet into his hands. Slowly, he dips his fingers into a clay bowl filled with almond oil and gently massages my ankles, my feet, my toes. Then he stops and just looks at me.

"This is enough for me now," he says. "Your feet are so beautiful."

I ask him about his marriage, but he won't talk about it. He just looks at the ground and shakes his head. Eighteen months ago, Ogin told me that Eitaro would always love me, but I didn't believe her. Now I see it is true.

I am feeling stronger now. I ask him if he has missed me. He says, "Yes, every morning and every night." I ask him why he didn't marry me. His eyes glaze over before he answers. His voice is filled with a quiet shame as he says, "It wasn't permitted."

I hate those words. I look away.

"My family would have disinherited me."

I feel the shadow again. The one that covered me eighteen months ago. Pain washes over me in a thick green wave — the sea water I thought I had escaped.

Eitaro tells me he will come again next Tuesday and lifts two boxes into my hands. They are wrapped in red paper with gold calligraphy. One has a silk kimono, purple with white gardenias. I rub the silk on my cheek, then wrap it around my shoulders. It fits perfectly. His fingers have an indelible kinesthetic memory. Yes, his hands have remembered everything. My mother couldn't have chosen it so well.

Something inside the boxes pulls us back through time. I am his ruby-throated hummingbird. I fly between rays of moonlight in his dreams. I sing to him from the humid center of the flowers. I am a persimmon in a red kimono, and he has come again to peel my petals. He says, "I want to be inside."

I look away. I'm drowning again in a tide of ocean water.

"I'm not in a hurry, Yukiko." I'm sure he can see the terror in my eyes. He says, "I'll wait."

The second box has a lacquer vase that he fills with white chrysanthemums. They are lovely, but he is eighteen months too late.

16

REFLECTION IN THE WATER

hen Kenji comes to see me again, I tell him about Eitaro. I ask him what to do, but he doesn't tell me. He won't. He can't. He tells me he lives in a different world, and I have to find my own way through mine.

I've lost my peace again, and the peace was so sweet.

There's something in his eyes that I haven't seen before. My eyes are full of questions. He doesn't have the answers, but his eyes are warm with a gentle heat. He pulls me close and wraps his robes around me. Even though I am confused, I feel accepted. This is something new.

"Kenji, I need your guidance."

"You don't need my wisdom, Yukiko. You need your own."

"But I can't find it right now."

"Then wait. Live with your questions for a while. Don't resist your confusion. Let its shadows and light wash through you. Let your questions flow through you like a river and carve their shape into your emotions. The answers you seek will come in time."

"But before the answers come..."

"Live at the edge of your questions. Don't resist them. They'll teach you what you need to know."

"But I feel like I'm drowning. What do I do while I'm tumbling underwater?"

"Paint the changing shapes of the current, and pay attention to your dreams. If a silver fish speaks to you, write down the message. If a blue fish swims to you, ask a question. If a lantern opens up a circle of light, paint what you see inside."

"But I want to know what to do right now."

"The only thing you can do is be patient and trust that the wisdom you need will come in time. Every time something needs to be born, whether it is a new soul or something new in you, a Birth Angel holds a lantern on your path. You have an angel guiding you right now, even if you can't see her. But sometimes she has to hold cotton wool over your eyes. If you knew everything ahead of its time, you couldn't learn from what you struggle with.

"Right now, your path is to keep walking in the dark, trusting what you can't see. I can see that you're walking on the razor's edge, but you won't fall off. You've gone too far already to stop.

"But let's paint now, Yukiko. The brushes are full of messages for you. The afternoon sun is slanting through your window, and the cicadas are singing to you from the other side of the pond."

"I don't know if I can paint right now. I feel too confused."

"Then stop thinking. Let the paint think for you."

Slowly and carefully, Kenji takes rice paper out of his

shoulder bag and mixes ink. He stops and studies me.

"I don't tell people what to do, Yukiko. I ask them who they are."

"The problem is I am too many people at the same time, fighting each other and swirling inside one body. I am a cloud inside a thunderstorm."

"Art can come out of that. We'll use the hoboku style of flung ink, like the ancient sumi-e masters. We'll let the shapes form themselves and tell their story."

I dip my brush in the ink and throw it at the paper. It splatters against a mountain and drips to the horizon.

"What does the ink tell you?"

"It tells me my life is like paint, and I have to let the shapes form themselves."

"What about the mountain?"

"That is where I dream."

"Your dreams will bring you messages."

I look up at Kenji. He takes my hand and presses it to his face. A soft kiss spreads like watercolors, ripples over a lake. Then he turns my palm up to the sky. Oh! He is painting my hand!

"My brush has a language for the day, a language for the night, and a language for my dreams. There is paint for rice paper and ink tones for the body — a language for the sculpture of your hands."

Now he moves the brush up my arms. The ink becomes birds, flowers, day and night. With slow, deliberate hands, he lifts off the silk of my kimono. Ink vines are climbing to my shoulders. Plum branches ripen around the half moons of my breasts.

His tongue brushes my nipples. Now he is painting a lake on my belly, a wild hoboku ink dance across my chest. My body is an ancient landscape, a dance of light and shadow, a spray of hibiscus, a wild dream forming itself until his mouth is home.

Kenji is the one at the edge right now. He is still a monk, and he has gone as far as I can let him. As lovers, we become what we want to be, but some things will always be a mystery.

After Kenji leaves, I study my reflection in the water. I have become a landscape, a lake, a flower, a river of dark and light. I light candles around my bed in a soft cocoon. The edges ripple in the light like fireflies.

Sometimes I am wise, and sometimes I am a thunderstorm. This is one of the mysteries of being a woman. Kenji belongs to the temple. I almost accept that he will never be mine, but part of me does not. Sometimes I want to be a goddess. Sometimes I want to reinvent the world.

17

THE GUARD AT THE TEMPLE

t's Tuesday, and Eitaro is here again. I don't completely know why, but I can't resist him now. Maybe it's because of my love for Kenji. I have kept Eitaro at a distance for eighteen weeks, but something inside me needs to love completely. It's been too long. This is something Kenji cannot do. It is forbidden.

I take him to the bath house, and Eitaro peels the red silk petals of my kimono. He covers me with kisses — my breasts, my shoulders, my arms, my fingers, behind my knees. He adores each one of my toes. And then he is inside me again, swimming home.

I feel like I am having a dream, but my eyes are open. We are in the bath house, surrounded by steam, inside a wall of tile as blue and mysterious as the late hours of the night on a new moon. And then, even though I am awake, the dream changes.

We are in a temple thousands of years ago in a different part of the world. I am a priestess and he is the guard at the temple. Our love is forbidden, but he is begging me to do it anyhow. He asks me to escape with him and go somewhere far away. We can travel in a boat or ride a camel, but I tell him this is forbidden.

When I finish my duties at the temple, he comes to me every night. He says that no one will see us, but I am afraid. I was consecrated to the Virgin Goddess as a very young child, and I serve her now. We are not allowed to love, and the punishment is death.

I am afraid the other guards have seen us. He asks me to run away again, but I am so afraid. I tell him it is forbidden. He has the camels ready, but it's so confusing. I love him, but I am a priestess. Two universes are pulling me at the same time. It's confusing, like being caught in the middle of a dust storm. Part of me goes one way, but part of me pulls somewhere else.

Two nights later the temple guards come for us, and I am surrounded with spears. The soldiers cover me with a linen robe and lead me through the fire. Then they tie my hands together and lower me into the tomb that has a mouth but no exit.

I am being buried alive. This is the last thing I remember before I am covered with sand.

18

AFTER THE
KAMO RIVER DANCES

 enji has come to see me again after the Kamo River Dances. He has been away for a long time. I ask him if he has missed me, and he says no. His words are an arrow through my heart, but he laughs and tells me I don't understand.

I ask him how his life is when he isn't with me. He laughs again. "I am a monk. I wake up before the birds and meditate until the sun is three fingers above the horizon. We gather together after that and chant sutras from Buddhist scripture. Then I go to the monastery kitchen, steam rice, cut vegetables, and make miso soup for our late morning meal. That is my work.

"In the afternoon I read scripture, practice calligraphy, paint my dreams, and find shapes with my brush for the visions I see in meditation. I show them to the Roshi and he guides me, the same way I guide you. In the late afternoon the monks gather in the temple to meditate. It's my favorite part of the day because time goes away. Then we eat in silence a simple meal of vegetables and brown rice, read scripture, and sleep."

He smiles. "But sometimes on a Thursday night, I take off my sandals, walk under the moonlight, and eat blackberries in the dream house. I have a sweet friend who lives there, a beautiful woman, and sometimes she gives me a bath. Sometimes more than that. Her skin is as soft as the blossom of an apricot, and her hands are the petals of a wild exotic flower. She is a mystery, and I love her deeply."

"But how can you love me and never think of me when you are away? This is something I don't understand. Don't you ever miss me?"

Kenji laughs again. "That would be a wrong understanding of time. It would violate my training. I am where I am at any moment in time."

He looks at me with his warm amber eyes and sees my confusion. A shadow has crossed my face. Two dragonflies have covered the pools that used to be my eyes. They have disturbed the water. Their wings are zig-zagging the air around my lantern with moving shadows.

He pulls me to his chest and wraps me in his arms until I am warm again. Then he takes my face in his hands and pulls my gaze up to his eyes. "You don't understand yet. Come back from where you are hiding and take my hands.

"Loving you has nothing to do with missing you. Loving is eternal. Missing is a wrong understanding of time. Some people think that time is horizontal, like a young deer crossing a pond from stone to stone. On one level of reality, that is correct. But time is also simultaneous."

Kenji's eyes are laughing, and maybe I am beginning to understand. His eyes are so warm, and his voice is silver. He runs his fingertips along my cheekbones, then traces the lines of my face. Now he is speaking to my heart.

"My love goes vertical in time. There's a huge powerful thing going on. There's an opening. There's a discovery, and it's amazing.

"We made a connection in the dream house, and there will be more. Loving you is easy. It's fun. It's joyous for me. When I'm with you, it's easy to love you.

"Loving you is an energy vortex. I'm not even going to think in advance what might happen. I want my love to be energy that flows through you and comes out of your mouth in words. I want my love to flow through your fingers and re-emerge in the sumi-e ink tones of your art. I want my kisses to enter your heart and flow up through your spine until time explodes through the top of your head and you are everywhere.

"You are the spark in the light of every one of the stars. You are the wind in the wings of every bird who knows freedom. You are the hands that wash my feet, the kisses that stain my lips with wild berries from the forest.

"When I'm away, I sometimes forget but I always come back. Don't ask me to miss you."

He laughs again, and this time I know he laughs because he's happy. He sees that I am beginning to understand. "And what is your life like when I am away?"

I smile — I am feeling stronger now. Before I speak, I pour jasmine tea into a raku bowl I made with clay from the river. I serve it to him and then I meet his eyes directly. "I am a geisha. I dance, I paint, I sing, I dream, I play the shakuhachi flute, and some things are a mystery."

19

THE MYSTERY HAS FLOWN

here's an ache I feel in my shoulder at night. It comes from the questions that nest in the hollow just below my right shoulder blade. This is the place on my body where your hand should be when I'm sleeping. But at least I'm not like the women who never let themselves love or dream.

I try to soothe the ache with my pillows. I arrange them in the shape of your body before I go to sleep. This helps in a small way.

I wonder if I will ever be with a man who is free to hold me through the night. I wonder what I would dream like that. Eitaro belongs to Izumi, and Kenji is a monk. He belongs to the Buddhist temple, and that's where he sleeps. I accept this, but I don't like it.

Kenji says his love goes vertical in time, but not horizontal. It's a good philosophy, but my heart has other plans. I just don't know how. Eitaro was a deeper mystery before he was married. The future was an open sky full of sunlight. We were both so innocent, full of love and longing, sweet like peaches ripening in the early summer. We never ate those peaches completely. I still enjoy Eitaro, but it's different now. Something is gone. The sky is smaller. The mystery has flown away.

If I were a rich man's wife, my husband would go to geishas. That sounds crazy. I wouldn't like it. But I am the geisha the rich men go to, and I don't like that either. My heart is looking for different wings.

But how do I find my way? I understand vertical love — I've had it twice now. But vertical love doesn't make the ache in my shoulder go away. I'm twenty-four years old, and I wonder if I'm doomed to sleep with pillows all my life.

I want to be held in the strong muscular arms of the man I love until doves sing in the morning. I want to dream inside the light where we both sleep until hummingbirds fly through the open windows. I want the sun to rise over Kenji's shoulders and warm his eyes until they flutter open. Yes, that's something I'd like to see — even once.

I want the ache in my shoulder to go away. I want the empty space to fill itself with light and the wings of monarch butterflies. But how? I still have to sleep with pillows instead of the sweet music of his hands.

20

A Different Smile

enji has come for my lesson on Tuesday, but I can't concentrate today. I haven't been able to sleep. At night my hair fills with blue swallowtail butterflies. They flutter in my dreams.

He pulls a book out of his satchel, but I don't want to read. I take it out of his hand and put it back in the bag by his feet. Then I fasten the straps. If he looks into my eyes, I'm sure he will see the whole story. I am silent — I keep it all in my eyes. Then the words pour out of me in a flood.

"I haven't been able to find the wisdom I'm looking for. Every part of my life is confusing. When I was in the forest last week, I drew a circle around myself and brushed my desires away from my feet with a straw broom. I played a wild melody to the birds with my flute. Then I brushed out the red maple leaves. Now I'm spinning in circles, and I don't even know what I want anymore. I can't sleep at night, and

63

I've forgotten how to dream.

"Maybe I've gotten too wild. Some of the people who come here to the teahouse are afraid of me. I can see it in their eyes. Last week, one of our dinner guests asked me to stop looking at him because my eyes were burning a hole in the back of his head. It was only a moment, but he couldn't stand it. I told him I didn't know what he was talking about, but it wasn't true. I started to play the flute, but then I couldn't stop laughing. You see, part of me laughs the way you do now.

"And I'm getting a boldness from I don't know where. This isn't in my training or my culture. After I finished my song, I watched him wiggle like a fish who is caught and frying at the bottom of a wok. It was so funny that I decided to add some vegetables and some spice.

"I have never entertained this man and I don't want to, but I decided to play with him. I said, 'Part of you wants to make love to me, and part of you is terrified. You have two voices now, and I want to hear words from both.'

"He said, 'I'd have to speak out of both sides of my mouth at the same time.'

"I smiled and said, 'Fine. Start talking.'

"He didn't know what to say. A woman had never spoken to him like this before."

Kenji is smiling a different smile than I have seen before. He looks suddenly older. He tells me, "There's something about you that's so innocent, and something that's older than your years at the same time."

"I thought I lost my innocence when Eitaro got married. I felt my dreams float out of my skin and find their home in Izumi's wedding slippers."

For a moment Kenji is lost somewhere, but then he comes back. "You don't lose your innocence, Yukiko. But you lose your faith that it can get you somewhere."

Sometimes I wonder where his wisdom comes from. Kenji has lived in the temple since he was six years old, but he seems to know more than his life could teach him there. Maybe his wisdom comes from somewhere else — another place and time.

Kenji's words pour into me like sunlight through an open door. His voice warms me. I don't know where the door is leading, but I know I have to trust him. He says I have to trust time too.

"Here's the good thing about your life. It took you to the edge. You see what you have and what you don't. Everything you knew took you to the edge of what you don't know. But Yukiko, that's a stunning place to be. Right now you're between the worlds. You will be living a different life when you get to the other side. All the teachers who guide you when you dream are going to help you. I am also here to help you."

"But how? You can't stay with me at night, and I want that more than anything."

"That's what you think you want, but there's something deeper that you want even more. That's where I am there for you completely — on the bridge between your past and something still unborn."

"But you don't understand! You're a monk, and you're not a woman!"

Kenji puts his finger softly to my mouth and draws a circle around the edges of my lips.

"For the next two weeks when you finish dancing at the teahouse, I want you to take out your flute and play a song to the moon. Don't play anything you have heard before. Each night play the music you hear in your heart. It doesn't matter if the song is happy or sad, as long as it is new. This will help you sleep again.

"Every night you will have a dream that will guide you

through a transition. Paint your dreams in the morning. I will come to see you again in two weeks, and you can show them to me.

"During these fourteen days the moon will disappear. Then it will be born in the early evening and start to grow again. When the light starts to come back, your innocence will be born again. Not like it was before, but in a different form. Something even better because you have more wisdom now."

This is a new idea for me. The seed of a flower growing through the edges of a stone. The stone is a pretty one I found at the ocean. I can hold it in my hand, but it will take time to grow roots there. I look at Kenji and study his face. So much peace there. So much light.

"I thought that my innocence was a moon that shattered in the sea. I thought it dissolved underwater and got eaten by the fish."

Kenji smiles. "Seven months ago, you watched your sister labor for three days and then give birth to her first child. For the next fourteen days, you will give birth to yourself."

I look at him, but suddenly I've forgotten how to speak. Nothing comes out of my mouth.

"You think you lost something two years ago, but actually it's the other way around. You have a strength, a wisdom, and a depth you didn't have before. Two weeks from now you'll have even more."

I still can't speak, but he holds me to his heart and I hear it beating. This is enough music for me right now. Then he combs my long black hair, first with my tortoise shell comb, then with his fingers. He doesn't stop until my pain disappears.

Kenji uncovers me petal by petal. Note by note. He speaks to all of the women who live inside me now and listens while

66

they sing their weaving songs, even if the harmonies clash sometimes. I am an innocent child, a mother at the edge of birth, a geisha, an angel, an ancient priestess, an old woman who lives alone in a hut on top of a mountain.

Now the sun is a fiery bird, singing yellow music in the branches of the late afternoon. Kenji has to leave. It's his hour of meditation.

I hold back my tears. "You're splitting me in half. You're pulling me between two worlds. Maybe I need to leave this life. Maybe I should be a Buddhist nun."

He pulls me close to him and kisses my hair. "You have to cut the rose with a knife before you can put it on your altar. Do you understand? Light your candles tonight and dream. Your dreams will heal you. And when you need to speak to me in that sweet and silent place that glows inside your own heart, I will be there."

After he leaves, I walk outside to the forest and swim in the river that has always been my friend. I rub my feet smooth with a rough-edged stone and let the sun dry my hair. Something in me feels old and new at the same time. But something in me has shifted, and I know I will dream again.

At night I put a beeswax candle in my lantern. I cut the paper shade over the candle into the shape of constellations until the room is filled with stars. As I put my wooden flute together, a musical voice tells me that each star is the shape of a dream.

Suddenly I am filled with a new song, and the notes flutter out of my mouth. The wind comes from all directions at the same time, and I breathe it into my flute. The shape of the music is wild, and it swirls around me before it flies out the window.

Before I sleep, I think of Kenji combing my hair, and my hair is wild with music. As he combs my hair, it fills with monarch butterflies. A veil is lifted away from my bare shoulders — first a ripple of yellow silk, then butterflies, then my hair. This is the first dream, but I still hear the music of an unfinished song.

21

CENTER OF
THE FLAME

 itaro has been gone for seven weeks, but he comes back with a razor. He asks me to hold it to his throat so he can watch me shave his face. I have been painting eggplants in dream colors and purple ink. The razor is like a bell too early in the morning. It is loud and difficult — like waking up from a disturbing dream. Or maybe the razor will tear a curtain to a room where everyone falls asleep.

He wants me to hold the razor to his throat while I love him. I am a geisha, and I wonder if being married makes people crazy. He says, "You have to see the silver and the work on the blade. There's poetry there."

I wonder if cold women make warm men lose their minds. This is a different Eitaro than I have ever known. Shaving a man who is halfway out of his mind wasn't part of my training. I have never shaved a man before.

Sometimes Eitaro can read my mind. His voice is strong.

He says, "I've been thinking about this every night for seven weeks. I want you to shave me. I am a tree with branches growing too far out of the garden. You can't understand a man until you scrape the bark from his face."

I am afraid, and he sees this in my face. "What if I make you bleed? What if my hand slips and I cut your throat?"

"If you make me bleed, it doesn't matter. I need you to change my face — to make it new again. To cover me with steam and soap, like a silkworm in a cocoon, so I can be reborn. If you cut my face, I'll wear the scar forever like a jewel."

I follow him on the stone steps to the garden. We walk across the pond, with jasmine floating through the humid afternoon air. The sun is hanging above the koi pond, ready to fall into the water. Soon it will be dark.

He watches me closely as I pick up the razor. I hold it to his throat. I hesitate.

He doesn't know if I am going to shave him or slit his throat. I don't know either. He watches me as time slows down, as the constellations dance in a slow circle across the sky. He knows there are things that I have never told him. He sees this in the blade of the knife.

He watches me as I study my reflection in the silver blade. As I run my fingers along the raw edge of my unanswered questions. The moonlight is streaming through the trees as jasmine petals fall on the stones outside. Then I start.

Pulling the blade across his face is like freeing the husk of a tree. I am in the middle of a wild forest, shaving bark. Something is changing inside me every second. My emotions swirl in a vortex that doesn't have a name.

"I want you to make my face new," he says.

I am at the edge — between the visible and the invisible. My voice is searching for words that don't have a language. Far better to stay in silence.

70

I hold the blade to his throat a second time, and he shivers. He doesn't know what I am thinking, and I can see a terror in his eyes. He doesn't know if it is day, or night, or a dream.

I pull the blade again. I am clearing a path in the forest. An open way inside a hedge of new pines. I am walking over the snow with Eitaro. Or is he walking with Izumi? Or am I walking with Kenji in the dark?

It is midnight, and I am walking through a fall of new snow. Or is it a candle? Am I walking to the center of a flame, a blade, or a face?

I put the blade to his throat and speak slowly. "Every time you come inside me, you hold a razor to my throat." I steady my hand. "If you want to love me tonight, you will be the one under the blade."

There is something in my eyes he has never seen before, and he doesn't know what it is. Neither do I. His eyes are full of questions, and his questions are out of control. Is it vulnerability, strength, or terror? Or is it a quiet peace hiding under a silver mask? My face is a thunderstorm, a lake with a small wooden boat before it is hit by lightning. He is the one who is sinking.

I break his silence. "Look at my face underwater."

Eitaro's body is pulsing with lightning. I am full of silver fish swimming to the moon — they swim in and out of his fingers. Now he is leaning into me, a silver fish in a shallow pond, then deeper. He teases me, dives to the edge, but he doesn't swim home.

I keep the razor at his throat. I am surprised at my own intensity as I tell him, "You know what it is like to be a woman now."

He whispers, "And you know how to hold me underwater."

The masks are gone now. We have turned each other

inside out. I look at my reflection in the water, but nothing is the way it was before. What has happened to my face? My eyes are changing every moment, and he is burning from inside. He is swimming in a lake that is hit by lightning.

What has happened to my face? I have become a thousand faces, each a butterfly with a different pattern on the wings.

I hold the razor to his throat. My voice is filled with a thousand birds flying in a maze of wings. "What have you done to me? What do you ask of me? Why have you come back into my life?"

It's almost like I am talking in a dream, and he doesn't listen. He is so far inside his own dream that he doesn't see the wings of mine.

He speaks softly, but his voice is strong. "I want to rub my new face next to your cheek. I want to breathe your breath, and I want you to devour me."

I keep the razor at his throat. I say, "If you want to love me, it will have to be like this."

I keep my hand on the blade as he comes inside me. I watch his face reflected in the silver as he plays me all the way to the razor's edge. Before I ripple, he hesitates, teases me, makes me wait, then swims home. The edges of my body become transparent, then they dissolve completely.

I am swimming to the moon, floating in a sea of wild orchids, running through the forest with white deer in the first rays of the morning. My eyes are changing every moment — chestnut eyes, eyes like almonds, eyes like waterfalls.

Now the moon is ten fingers into the sky. I light a row of candles and watch them glow in the reflection of the water in the garden. Then the silver captures me again. What has happened to my face? In the dance to the razor's edge, my face has changed.

22

TO LOVE
IN FREEDOM

ometimes I talk with the guests at the teahouse about their wives. I wish they would talk to their wives the way they talk to me.

Takashi has been married for almost ten years. He has two lovely children, a boy and a girl. His wife is beautiful but uneducated. He says there is something about being married that makes him feel obligated to love her in a certain way. "Obligated," he says. "I hate that. It isn't happy. It takes away my freedom."

I laugh. "So that's why you come to geishas."

"I like it here because there aren't any rules. The women here understand me. I can love Satomi or Hiroko for an evening and then go home. I'm not obligated. I don't lose my freedom."

"Can't you love your wife too?"

"It's different, and I don't know how to explain. It's something about men that's difficult for women to understand."

73

"I don't understand anything about being married. I'm a geisha. I've been in love twice, but it hasn't been like that. My parents were married, but they sent me here for my education at an early age. I don't know a different life. I know music, dancing, and poetry. Marriage is a mystery to me — something beyond the beyond."

"Yukiko, your way is better. You can love in freedom."

I feel like I am spinning inside a cloud. Eitaro saw me like this in one of his dreams. I was whirling in a red kimono. I stopped spinning suddenly, whispered something to him, and then dissolved into a cloud of blue and yellow butterflies. Eitaro still won't tell me what I said.

You can love in freedom — what exactly does this mean? And what is marriage to a geisha? Eitaro got married and went away for eighteen months. Then he came back. Kenji adores me, but he sleeps in the Buddhist temple. It seems I have to find a different way.

"Yukiko, come back! Your face is in a cloud. Where are you swimming?"

"Maybe you can explain a few things to me."

"Then you'll have to step out of the cloud and talk to me."

Satomi comes to our table with two cups of sake and an iris. I take them off the tray and tell her not to worry with my eyes. This doesn't seem to help so I excuse myself. Behind the painted screen I tell her, "You don't have to worry. Takashi and I are only talking."

"I don't like it."

"Satomi, we're only talking and you can have him later. I have other plans." My plans are to play the flute and paint, but she wouldn't understand.

"I don't like it when he talks to other women."

"Satomi, we are geishas, and we don't own anyone. I was talking to him about that."

"But Takashi loves me."

74

"That doesn't mean you own him. He's married — whatever that means. I'm trying to find out."

"He and I don't talk about it."

"No?"

"It's something I'm trying to forget."

"Maybe you should look it in the face."

"It's too hard."

"He needs to talk right now — about that."

"I know, and I can't."

"Then let him talk to me. I'll bring him to you later."

I bow to her and walk back to Takashi, holding an iris. I put it in the vase. Maybe I will put my flute together and play him a song, but he stops me.

"Satomi loves me and she's very sweet, but I feel obligated. She's not even my wife, and I feel obligated. I hate that. I want to love in freedom."

"Why is obligated the way to feel when someone loves you? Why not just dive in and get lost?" I'm getting bold again. I don't know where it comes from, but I like the way it feels.

"That's my problem. I can't get lost."

"Close your eyes for a moment, and imagine something beautiful. A dancer, a nightingale, or a silk pillow. Whatever you see in your vision, walk into it and get lost."

"I'm trying, but there's an edge there."

"The edge is where God is."

Takashi opens his eyes and he looks confused. Sometimes I have to remember that I'm not talking to Kenji. Takashi is different. He doesn't think about these things.

"I don't know about God. For me, that's beyond the beyond. But let's talk about Satomi and Hiroko. I love women. When I'm inside them, I don't think about the future."

"You're afraid of the future."

"It's something I just don't like to think about."

"Wanting something and not wanting something are opposite ends of the same cage. They both lead to pain. Did you ever think about that?"

A cloud crosses his face but it clears quickly. He tells me I'm beautiful and different from other women.

"If you don't want to talk about the future, you can comb my hair."

"Your hair is so shiny, long and black."

"I'll take the combs and flowers out. You can use my comb or your hands, but be careful. Sometimes my hair fills up with butterflies."

"I'll let them fly through my hands."

Takashi combs my hair, and this feels good to me. I close my eyes and think about Kenji. But there are more words inside me, and they come tumbling through my mouth.

"I have to say this because we are running out of time. Sometimes you have to live at the edge of your questions. Sometimes you have to feel your way in the dark with your hands.

"There are times when life cracks you open so raw, it's almost hard to breathe. But if you keep the edges raw, you can see the forces of nature and accept their power. This is God's way of showing you that He's behind the veil. Sometimes you have to love what you can't understand. Life can be confusing, and sometimes you have to honor the mysteries.

"You don't have to live like an animal in a cage. There are other ways to think and be, even if you don't know them yet. For example, you can choose to be in love with your wife. It's an option. Even if you have to pretend she's a geisha.

"Or you can choose to love Satomi in freedom, even for a night. She's waiting for you now."

23

FILLED WITH
MOONLIGHT

 ometimes my voice is a bird weaving through the forest. She's yellow, but she doesn't have a name. I write the pictographic shapes of my voice in calligraphy on rice paper. I draw the moon through layers of bamboo, brush blossoms on a branch of hibiscus, and uncover a secret landscape I see only in my dreams.

But I want to paint something different now. A dragon or a human body. I don't know how to do that yet. It would involve a translation to paint of what I see with my hands. The paint would have to start with touch, then move through the eyes, and back to a world of light and shadow.

Poetry is easier sometimes. I like being made love to with words. I like the way they swirl around me and take their shape in my fingers. Or in the shape of your mouth behind my knees. Sometimes language clears the path for its own intention, the way a dream can reshape a life.

I paint the way I touch you in the moonlight. This isn't something I can explain with words. I can only do it with my hands or in the cryptic language of a dream. The dream could become a poem. The man would be in the soft skin of the letters, and she would feel it whenever she wanted him to caress her.

I want to paint Kenji's words in moonlight around his body. I want to paint the shape of his voice. His voice saying, "When you touch me, it's like going through the moon." I see him in the forest walking through a tangle of branches. I paint him in sumi-e colors, layers of ink on skin, moon brushed. The moon swims out of his skin like flying fish through a silver tunnel.

My mouth is filled with moonlight until every part of your body is loved and touched. The sky is ink and your face is rising over the eastern mountains. Your mouth is filled with a sacred language, syllables you sing to me over and over while we are making love. I want you to love me with paint until my shoulders are filled with moonlight.

My edges are translucent. My kisses touch you like violets in a light rain.

24

FLOWER AND
WILLOW WORLD

 itaro has come back to the geisha house to drink forbidden love, and he says he wants me to have his child. I tell him he's out of his mind, but I have to sit down before I stop breathing. I wonder if he can see the terror in my eyes.

Everything in the room is a blur, and I am ten different women at the same time. The women are swans on the same lake swimming in ten different directions. I try to pull them back.

Eitaro asks me to think about it. It's a strong desire, and he has decided that it's a good idea — for both of us.

I turn to face him directly. "No, Eitaro. My answer is no."

"Why, Yukiko? We talked about this before, and it was something both of us wanted. You wanted it too, as much as I did, maybe even more."

"That was a long time ago."

"Yukiko, you have always wanted children. This is what

I want too. Our children will be beautiful, and they will be able to sing and dance like you. I saw this in a dream."

"You are married, Eitaro. Have your children with your wife. It will be better that way."

"She cannot. Her belly has been flat since our wedding day."

"Go see the midwives. They have herbs that can help you with this."

"We have. The herbs didn't work, and Izumi won't even let me come to her futon anymore."

"I don't want to be anyone's second choice."

"You're not. But it took me this long to understand that I really could have my children with you."

"This isn't something I want anymore. There was a time that I did, but that time is gone."

"Think about it, Yukiko. Talk to your womb. Ask her if she wants to fill herself with children. I think she does. I made a wrong decision two years ago, but that time is gone. What you have always dreamed about is possible now."

"And where will I live when I have this baby?"

"Here in the geisha house."

"No, that's not my way. I may be a geisha, but some things about me are very traditional."

"There are many geisha women who have children with their lovers. I talked to Okasan about it."

"My answer is no."

"I will take care of you, Yukiko. I will give you everything you need. Everything."

"I will not have a baby in the geisha house. Right now I am an artist in the flower and willow world, but a child needs a mother, a father, and a home."

"Just think about it, Yukiko. Take your time. I have always loved you and I want you to have my children. I love you, Yukiko. Try to understand."

I have to sit down again. The room is spinning like a typhoon. What kind of crazy love is this that twists itself into my heart out of time?

I gather my strength again for a few moments. "And if I agree to your plan, you'll leave your wife to take care of me when my birth time comes?"

"Of course, Yukiko."

"What if the birth takes three days? My sister's did."

Eitaro doesn't know how to answer me now, and I am starting to lose control in a way beyond anything I have let myself feel before. I am a thunderstorm, and I am gone.

"It's too late," I shout at him. "Too late now. You should have thought of this before."

"How could I know back then? I was a boy. I was still a child."

"You traded a store full of silk for the river of birth. You traded money for your unborn children. Go away from me!"

"I love you, Yukiko. I have always loved you."

Eitaro has tears in his eyes, a rain I have never seen before. But I am a thunderstorm over the Kamo River, and the flood won't stop. The thunder has to clear before I can speak again, but my words are softer now. "I honor you, Eitaro, but what you desire is a door in the past that is frozen. It's too late now — the door is gone. There's so much about me now that you don't even know."

"Yukiko, I never wanted to hurt you."

"But you did, Eitaro. More than you ever knew."

We gaze at each other for a long time, the way monks do when they are trying to understand a deeper truth. For a few moments the masks are gone. His eyes are so vulnerable, full of the weather of sorrow and pain and longing.

Suddenly I am filled with compassion. Eitaro is putting himself on the thin edge of a high branch on a winter tree.

I think about shaving him again, shaving bark. I look at his eyes through time and see the vulnerability there. I wasn't aware of that before. I remember some of the wishes I buried under snow because I thought they were impossible. I look at his face, and in the reflection I see inside his eyes, I see mine. The light in the room is softer, but my emotions are ankle deep in broken glass.

"Eitaro, I want to tell you about the time we were apart. It was very hard at first, and my heart was filled with broken glass. But over time the pain became a blessing. I learned how to paint during that time, and I also learned about myself in ways I didn't know before. For many months I lived in a space that was empty. It was like the hollow center of a tree. A place where the owl lives, but the owl was gone. My heart was an empty room. But then the empty space began to vibrate, fill with light, and give birth. I didn't give birth to a baby, but look at the sumi-e shapes on the rice paper all around you. All of these paintings are mine. I'm living a new life now."

I gaze at the man in front of me, the sweet persimmon of my first love. He looks softer now, but I can see from his eyes that he doesn't understand. His eyes are so warm they melt me, but I have changed. I need more than that now.

"Yukiko, you seem the same to me. Sweet and loving, as always."

"That's why I can't have your baby. I live in a world that you can't see. I paint my walls with colors hidden from your eyes."

"I want to see. I'll try to see."

"Right now, I almost wish you could, but your life follows a different river."

"Yukiko, you have always wanted a baby. We talked about it so many times. We dreamed about it together."

"But then you went away and hurt me more than you

knew or cared at that time." Now I think I'm in trouble. The room is spinning. I am becoming a thunderstorm again.

"Yukiko, that's over now. It's in the past. We can have the baby."

"And your marriage?"

"That doesn't matter."

"It matters to me. It's too late now."

"Yukiko!"

"Go away! Go away!"

I am completely out of control. I am screaming at the top of my voice, and I can't stop. Okasan rushes in, then my sisters. I collapse into their arms, and I can't stop shaking.

Eitaro looks at me with the saddest eyes. He tries to calm me, and his voice is so soft. "Please, Yukiko. Please!"

My heart is filled with sorrow, but I can't do this anymore. I have to tell him.

"Go away, Eitaro. Don't come back. The time for us is over now. Go back to your wife, or find someone else to love."

25

A Tunnel
of Dark Wind

omehow Kenji has gotten the message to come to the teahouse. Maybe a hummingbird whispered it in his ear, or maybe the dark side of the moon entered the sky of his dreams. I cannot speak to him about what happened, and he doesn't ask. He combs my hair until I become a waterfall.

Nothing in my life is the way it used to be. I'm totally inside out. The space where my old ideas used to live is empty. I feel like I don't weigh as much as I did a week ago. I've lost a layer of moonlight around my breasts, my face, and over the bones of my hips. Kenji says I'm wearing my grief on my body. He says he'll comb my hair until the weight comes back.

Something has died that wasn't ever born, and I don't know how to live with this. This isn't anything I can dream about or paint. Maybe there are invisible cords tying me to Eitaro and the children we never had. A tunnel of dark wind for grief to pour through.

At least Kenji doesn't ask me to speak. That's more comfortable right now. He massages my back, my head, and my shoulders. Kenji has always known how to touch me, and when to be silent.

Last night I dreamed about a silver bowl — large, perfectly round, very thin silver, no edge. In back of that, the sky all around, with the constellations floating. A thin edge of light at the horizon.

My edges are transparent. Everything that has happened in my life is washing through. I am an open canvas, and everything I see, feel, taste, touch, and dream is becoming a part of me.

Life is the paint, and the edges bleed through. Joy bleeds through. Pain bleeds through — it doesn't matter. I am at the far edges of vulnerable. I can't resist anything anymore.

26

KANNON, GODDESS OF COMPASSION

 don't know what is wrong with me, but I haven't been able to speak for two weeks. I haven't been able to sleep or paint or dream. I lie on my bed and look up at the ceiling. When people talk to me, I can hear them, but I can't say anything back.

My sisters come to my room and feed me. I know they cook the meals themselves. There's so much love in the food that it makes me weep. Sometimes I smile at them to let them know I feel their love, but I don't have any words. My mouth is a dovecote. The eggs are broken. The doves have flown away.

Okasan comes to stay with me whenever she has time. Even though I can't speak to her or anyone, she holds me close to her and tells me stories. I am her favorite child, and she is Kannon, the Goddess of Compassion. She sleeps in my room and brings me tea in the morning.

Okasan folds me into the soft, womanly curves of her

87

love. She tells me I am the best persimmon tree in her garden, and in the spring the fruit will come back. Every day she massages me. I love this, but my voice doesn't come back. Maybe this is because it's still winter.

A few days later I hear Okasan talking to my sister. She says I am trapped in a silk cocoon, and she doesn't know which herbs to use for this kind of birth. She will go to Kenji.

27

PATH BY THE KAMO RIVER

hen Kenji comes back on Tuesday, he carries a woven cloth and asks me to fill it with whatever I will need for two cycles of the moon.

"I talked to Okasan and asked her if I could take you to live with the Buddhist nuns at the Temple in Sagano. She knows that you have always been different from the other geishas. She thinks a change will be good for you right now, and she said yes."

I look up from the blue silk pillow where I am sitting. I bite my lip. I want to say something, but the words don't come. There is only the confusion in my eyes.

"It won't be forever, Yukiko. Just for a while, until you feel like yourself again. You can take your flute, your paint, and your dreams. I think you'll be happy there. The nuns will treat you like a sister. You can meditate with them, live a simple life, and listen to the river when you sleep. It will be a special time for you, away from the world. Will you go with me?"

I still can't speak, but I nod my head. Behind Kenji's shoulders a river breeze is weaving through the paper lanterns of the teahouse. Soon I won't see them anymore.

An hour later, Kenji and I are walking on the path by the Kamo River. Most of the time I follow him, but for a few moments when nobody else can see us, he holds my hand.

28

A DIFFERENT LIFE

y life with the Buddhist sisters is simple and sweet. We get up with the sun and meditate as the light grows into morning. We grow kabochas, burdock, and apricots in the garden by the temple wall and cook together in the kitchen. Simple meals of vegetables and brown rice. The temple is filled with such a deep silence and so much peace that I drink it even in the soup we have for our evening meal.

Anjusama, the head of the order, has an ancient face. Her eyes remind me of Buddhist sculpture in temples I visited as a child. Her smile is serene and loving, and her cheekbones are wide and open like the forest. She cares for all of us like a mother, but it's different because her love is so spiritual.

In my free time I walk barefoot on the paths by the Kamo River. Then in the late afternoon the sisters chant from Buddhist scripture. I like to listen. Something about this life is so familiar. It's almost like living on a branch of a tree that grows in a different part of time. If I look out of my window at night, I can see the paper lanterns of the teahouses of Gion waving in the distance, but their colors don't pull me. The humid air between us is a pillow for my emotions. I'm living a different life.

The best part is that the sisters never ask me to speak. I live in a world of silence. My words are still plovers that have flown away. They haven't come back. But at night I have started to dream again, and I know this is a good omen. Sometimes my dreams are so dark that I don't want to remember them in the morning. I don't understand why I have to keep looking at everything that has hurt me. It's a painting in midnight ink that I want to run from, but it keeps repeating. I want to change these images into birds, then open the slats of my window and let them fly away.

But sometimes when I sleep, my teachers come to me. This is why I'm not afraid to dream anymore. We walk together along a path of yellow leaves to a sacred mountain. The moonlight streams through the branches over our bare feet as we walk on winding paths and bridges over rivers. We light candles at altars of flowers inside long rows of stone lanterns, each one a different color. After many hours of walking, they take me to a hidden place where they teach me. Then I dissolve and I am home.

I start to paint before I start to speak. I carry a basket to the river every afternoon with rice paper, ink, brushes, and my poems. Many weeks go by, and I almost feel peaceful in this life. In my silence. One afternoon when the season begins to get warmer, Anjusama follows me down to the river. She asks me what I have in the basket. First I show her my paintings, and she looks at them deeply. Her eyes and her concentration remind me of Kenji. Also her peace.

"And what else?" she says.

I answer in calligraphy. "I've written a book of poems called *Blackberries in the Dream House*. Maybe they will be published one day. After I die."

She reads the poems slowly and tells me they are beautiful. I see so much love in her eyes that I feel at peace. Then we gaze at each other — this is a Buddhist form of meditation. Now I see something else in her eyes, and it flutters out of her mouth. "Yukiko, we have all respected your silence. We have honored you and given you many weeks of quiet time for meditation, but now it's time to speak."

I want to obey her. I try to move my mouth, but I can't. The plovers are crippled. The words won't come out.

She seems to understand. "Your mouth is a bird that has forgotten how to sing, but it's a temporary amnesia. Deep inside she knows, and we're going to find your voice again."

I try to speak again, but I can't. I want to ask her how.

She knows. "Yukiko, there's more to our life here than scripture and meditation. Everyone has an individual path and private work to do on her own. Spiritual work. I see that you are getting stronger. I see a growing peace in your eyes, but you can't keep running away from your nightmares. Sometimes you have to dream them out loud."

She points to the district of Gion beyond the wooden fence around the temple garden. "Many people there are living nightmares because they're running away from their lives and running away from their dreams. But a few people have chosen a different path — like you right now. Yukiko, it's time for you to turn around, face your nightmares, and walk through them.

"I know something happened before you came here. I don't know what it is and you don't have to tell me, but I can feel it all around you and see it in your face. You've had your time to rest and that was good. It was necessary. But now it's time to let the loss transform you. I know it's a wild forest, but you can only see the path from the center. Let yourself feel everything. That's the only way you can walk through.

"As Buddhists, we accept everything — night and morning, heat and cold, joy and sorrow. The spiritual center of everything is the same. You are a living, breathing sculpture of one of the faces of God, and these are the stones on the river that shapes your soul."

We walk together for a way on the path by the river before she continues speaking. I watch a row of cranes fly south across the sun. Then she continues to instruct me. "Don't try to run away from anything, Yukiko. You can't. Let the salty waves of the ocean wash green water over you. Let the wind blow its music into your bones. It doesn't matter if the melody is happy or sad, as long as it's your own. Feel the alone. Feel the empty. Trust the alone and let it work in you. The empty space is what creates the new.

"You're still high in the mountains, but you're only part way on your journey home. And I want to tell you a secret. Obstacles aren't endings — they're blessings from God to point you in another direction. Every ending is always a beginning. Confusion is always a door to something new. Trust the light that brought you to this place to keep guiding you on your journey. Yukiko, you are a bright soul. Your light will reignite the spark that sings its fire in you."

This is a lot to understand in one afternoon. It feels good in my heart, but my legs are shaking. I need to sit down on a rock by the river and watch the water flow. Anjusama sits with me for a while, but then she speaks again.

"For the next two weeks, I want you to paint all of your dreams, including your nightmares. And keep on writing poems. The dark poems are missing from your book, and we live in a world of light and shadow. As Buddhists, we embrace them both.

94

"I want you to find a place in your poems for all of the emotions that live in you, all of the goddesses who breathe your name. I know there are many women who swim in your emotions. Each of them has a name and a voice. Let all of these goddesses speak, and listen carefully to what they have to teach you. Let them be as wild and fierce as a caged animal searching for freedom. Let them be soft and sweet as a lover. Let them be wind and rain and snow. Whatever the voices demand. Take each voice to the edge, and then even further. This is the way you open your heart to the world until everything inside of you, everything you hear and see, everyone you meet is speaking to you.

"The voice inside the fire will come first. Then the voice of the wind and the voice of the water. Give each voice a painting and a poem. Then you will swim through the moon and find the silent lake where the compassionate voice breaks through."

We sit in silence and listen to the river now. A hummingbird hovers over my shoulder, then flies away to a green collage of emerging leaves. The birds in the forest have always been my friends.

"One more thing, Yukiko. When you find the compassionate voice, remember to be compassionate with yourself."

I smile and nod my head.

In the distance one of the sisters is ringing the gong to gather for chanting scripture. Before we walk up the path from the river, Anjusama gazes at me. "Trust the empty place, Yukiko. It's the place where the new is born." She takes my hand. "Bring your basket of dreams, and we'll walk together again in a week."

29

BROKEN WING
OF AN ANGEL

There's a broken wing of an angel on my bedroom floor. It hardened into glass when the sun rose in the morning, splintered all over the room, and one of the thin glass bones pierced the bottom of my foot — the part I need to dance.

The Buddhists say that we are all created with a spark of the divine, and our thoughts, dreams, emotions, even our bodies, hover around the spark. We spin like planets around an elliptical orbit, and then, before we are born, harden into shells around the fire. The wild language of our dreams, the fire of our emotions, the tears of our transitions, and the soft kinesthetic mystery of our skin are all gifts from the spark — a minotaur's maze designed to open the way back home.

Before I sleep every night, I light a beeswax candle. The light is soft, and it takes away some of the fear. I am still afraid to sleep because of my nightmares. The flame is a glowing mystery without boundaries, hovering over a tiny lake of beeswax. The light warms my hands, and it helps with the transition. But not with the dreams. At midnight I'm spinning so fast that I don't know how to fall, and something inside me is afraid to burn.

The angels speak to me in familiar voices. "Keep on walking in the dark. Follow the fireflies until you fall asleep in a meadow of hibiscus. The fireflies will tell you secrets. Even if you have walked barefoot in the snow, it's getting warmer now. Feel the alone. Love the empty place inside of you until it starts to hum and glow. That's the ripple where you'll feel your future."

Every transition is blind, and when the rope bridge crosses a river you can't see, you have to feel your way with your hands. I still hear Okasan's voice saying, "Keep spinning until you leap into the unknown. Don't be afraid to fall — someone will catch you."

Maybe the one who catches will be my own hand. Or maybe someone I wasn't able to see well enough before — someone who walks out of the shadows. A dance partner who lifts me over his shoulders.

I've lost the lantern I carved with the shapes of the constellations. Maybe it shattered like an angel of glass in an abandoned window. But as she falls to the floor, she whispers, "Sometimes gifts from the angels come in splinters."

I can't see my future, but I'm creating myself every day — even if my foot is still bleeding. I let my hair spin until it's wild, and circle around whoever is in front of me, gypsy style.

Part of me is still afraid, and the path I walk in the dark is full of mud that sticks between my toes. But as I am walking, the deer push their brown heads softly into mine and suck my fingers. They pull off my obi and fill me with the soft scent of morning, even if the spark is still hiding.

30

PEBBLES FROM
THE RIVER

 notice something changing inside of me. The place in me that was damaged has become empty. Slowly, it is beginning to vibrate and glow. The empty space has been filling up with nightingales that fly in and out of my sleep. They fill my throat with song.

By the river I start to sing again before I start to speak. I sing to the birds in the forest, and they sing back to me. I am learning the melody of each of their songs. Sometimes I answer with my flute and sometimes with my voice.

I had nightmares for almost a week after I talked with Anjusama. They came like twigs in the wind from everywhere in time. When I was afraid to sleep, I listened to the river. But as hard as it was to walk those deserted paths, I knew the visions I saw were healing me. The second week some of my dreams became clear again. Washed in watercolors. Washed in moonlight with the river running through.

Before we walk to the river, Anjusama and I meditate together in the temple. I leave flowers at the feet of Buddha. Then I gather my dreams in a basket and follow her down the path to the river.

We sit together under the shade of a persimmon tree and listen to the river. I love the music of the ripples over stones. It's so peaceful. The birds sing to us, and I answer them with my flute.

Anjusama studies me. "Now answer them with your voice."

I begin to sing. First the song of the nightingale. Then the plover. Then the sparrow and the lark.

"Now tell me about the dreams in your basket."

I look up at her from where I am sitting on a rock. I wonder if I can.

She smiles like Kenji. "Last night when I was sleeping, I visited your teachers. They all told me that it's time."

I bow to her. She is my teacher too.

At first it is difficult to form my thoughts into syllables. They get stuck in my mouth. It feels like my mouth is filled with pebbles from the river, but somehow the words find their way out. At first I speak slowly and softly, as Anjusama reassures me with her eyes.

I tell her about my nightmares, but I tell her about other things too. The voice inside the waterfall. The silver bowl with the edge so thin it cuts the face of the moon. The messages from the lantern fish. The shape of things unformed. Then we hear the gong from the temple drifting through the leaves. It's time to walk up the path again.

31

A WORLD
OF SILENCE

I walk with Anjusama every Tuesday, and now I speak with the other sisters too. We sing when we plant kabochas and melons in the garden, and I entertain them with stories as we cut our vegetables for soup. Most of the stories make them laugh. Maybe I'm acting like a geisha again.

Also, I have been dreaming about Kenji. I wonder what he paints and what he dreams. I almost remember his hands, his back, and his shoulders, but from here it seems like a different life, something far away.

This is a very different life than when I was with the geishas. In the geisha house there are rules for everything. How to speak, how to serve tea, how to pour saki, how to perform the traditional dances, when to sing, and when to keep silent. And the most important rule — don't show your emotions, and never fall in love with a client. It isn't real. I don't want to live like that anymore.

101

At the same time, without the rules I feel so vulnerable. The tiniest thing can set me off, and I'll want to stop speaking again. Even if I just imagine it. Even if I know that what I imagine isn't real. It was easier to live in a world of silence. It wasn't so close to the edge.

My life is still different in certain ways from the other sisters. I haven't taken vows, so I didn't shave my head. Anjusama doesn't know if I'm going to stay here or not, so we're waiting for the answer to come from inside. My hair is still long, but I don't pin it up with combs anymore. I braid my hair or wear it long and wild. There is so much beauty here, in the birds, in the trees, in the river, in the eyes of every sister, that I don't miss the silk of my kimonos. My simple cinnamon robe gives me much more joy.

I'm happy here in the Buddhist temple. It's a sweet and simple life. It's an open life, and I almost feel at peace. I wonder if I should stay here always, and I fall asleep with this question.

32

SUN AND MOON, STONE AND RIVER

njusama comes to find me in the morning. She knows I've had a vision in the small hours of the night. She looks at me with her female Buddha eyes. Eyes that ask, "What did they tell you last night?" Eyes that say, "You can trust me."

"They told me it's time to leave the Buddhist temple." Already, I have so many tears in my eyes.

"Who told you?"

"The Snow Angels and all my teachers."

"And why?" Her eyes are so calm, so reassuring. She watches me swim from the deep lake in the center of her inner peace.

"My teachers say I am strong enough to be out in the world again. And the Snow Angels tell me that the life of a Buddhist nun isn't what they have planned for me this time."

"They told me also. But I had to make sure that you were

clear enough to hear their voices too."

"They said this time in the temple was planned for me before I was born, and that the events that led me to follow Kenji up the river were all necessary to bring me to this gate. They said that when I leave, my life will be different, almost as though I've been reborn."

"That is correct. Your life will surprise and delight you in many ways. Everything will be new."

"I don't want to live the way I did before."

"And you won't. Inside, you are very different now, even more than you realize. What is inside you will bring you peace and show you different ways, even if your outer life is much the same."

"I don't like the rules of the geisha world."

"You hardly followed them before."

Now we are both laughing, and my joy is filling the room again. My joy is a silver carp swimming in the deep lake of my older sister's silence. But suddenly a cloud shadows the water.

I gaze at Anjusama until I am lost in her eyes. My edges dissolve until I'm back in the silence that makes me strong.

My words are like my newly acquired self-confidence, delicate at the edges but strong inside. "I don't want to hide my emotions anymore. I don't want to pretend I am someone I'm not. And I want to be everything I am as a woman. All the colors flowing inside my paintbox. All the stops open on my flute."

Anjusama is smiling as I continue. "I need to hope what I hope, and dream what I dream without any boundaries. Sun and moon, stone and river, light and shadow. Geisha or no geisha, I have to be all I am as a woman now."

Anjusama takes my hand and leads me to the altar. We light candles and offer flowers to the lotus feet of the Buddha. I feel like he is holding me in his arms. Then, one of the sisters taps the gong, and we meditate into the silent hours of the late afternoon. I have never felt so much peace.

Before our evening meal, Anjusama takes my hands. "Yukiko, you are a sweet and beautiful soul, full of art and full of light. We all love you deeply, and you have our blessings. I want you to know you will always be welcome here, but this isn't your home. You don't have to leave before you are ready, but both of us know it's getting close to the time. I want you to know that when you leave, you will carry our voices with you. Also our love."

33

BASKET
OF DREAMS

he sun rises over the plum trees in the garden on my last morning in the Buddhist temple. Last night I had a vision of Kannon, the Goddess of Compassion. She walked with me from a row of temple candles at the feet of Buddha to a string of paper lanterns on the balcony of a geisha house. Then she smiled at me and said, "It's all the same."

When I leave the temple this afternoon, I know that she will be walking with me. The best part is I feel like myself again, even more than that. I have no idea what is coming, but I'm ready to go back.

In certain ways it's a morning like any other. I join the sisters for morning meditation, my routine for many months now. But when I get back to my room, I know that time is an edge that is changing. I'm leaving a time that has been very soft and healing to me, and I won't be coming back.

I put on my blue silk kimono and tie the obi around my

107

back. Time is moving softly like the waves in the Kamo River, but part of me wants the river to stop. I gaze at my tiny wooden room, the tatami on the floor, and the branches of the plum trees through the slats of my window. I gaze at the flowers in the temple garden. Part of me wants to become a twig of bamboo.

But the river keeps moving as the sun lifts higher and higher into the morning sky. Slowly and carefully, I fold the clothes that I brought here many months ago when I walked the path by the Kamo River. It feels like folding origami paper cranes. The wings fold together, and everything fits into the furoshiki. I gather my gifts from Anjusama and my sisters — a bronze statue of Buddha, incense tied with a ribbon, and ten candles. I hold these gifts close to my heart.

Before I depart, we have a meal together. Miso soup, vegetables, and brown rice. Then the nuns stand around me in a circle, holding candles. One by one, I bow to each of the sisters. We bless each other with our hands and our eyes. Then I fold the simple robe they gave me months ago and give it back to Anjusama. Cinnamon in the Holy Mother's hands.

For a few moments, doubts about what I am doing flash across my eyes. I've been inside a cocoon, and I have no idea what is coming next or how my life will be on the other side of the river. I don't even know if I want to walk there now.

As always, Anjusama reassures me with her eyes. "Sometimes important changes happen in silence. You only notice how different you have become later. I don't know how it will be for you, Yukiko, but I do know that you'll be fine."

One by one, the sisters leave for their afternoon tasks. I watch their feet disappear into the light as they walk out the door. I listen to their sandals on the slate stones of the path, until even the sound disappears into silence.

I carry a basket of flowers, and I leave petals inside the

row of candles at the feet of the Buddha. Then I fold my hands, honor the silence of the room, and say good-bye.

In the early afternoon, I put on my sandals. Then I walk up the path by the river with my basket of dreams.

34

THE WILD AND MYSTERIOUS ONE

hen I walk into the teahouse, Okasan is waiting for me on the other side of the door. She folds her kimono-covered arms around me. Then she invites me into her sitting room for a formal tea ceremony and welcomes me home as her daughter. She tells me how much she has missed me and how glad she is to have me back. Then she takes my hand to walk with me to my new home.

She has a room ready for me in back of the geisha house, next to the garden. "This is perfect for you, Yukiko. It will be quiet and sweet like your room in the Buddhist temple."

When I sit and close my eyes, I can hear the music of the Kamo River rippling over the tumbling stones. This is reassuring. Okasan has filled the room with irises and silk. I drink in the colors with my eyes and run my fingertips along the softness of my new kimonos. I don't really know how long I've been away, and all of this almost feels like a

111

dream. But even if it is a dream, it's a happy one.

We sit in silence for a while. I brush my face softly against the petals of the flowers, let the sun warm my smile. I put on my sandals and walk around the garden. The songs of the birds are the same as the birds in the woods by the Buddhist temple, but something is different that I don't completely understand. Maybe the distance I've walked is further than the path up the river.

Okasan sits in silence and watches me. Then she breaks the silence with news about my geisha sisters. Two new maiko have come to the teahouse, and one of them has a beautiful singing voice. The other is the daughter of a Kabuki actor. Hiroko has moved to Osaka with a wealthy patron, and Satomi is expecting a child.

Something about this pulls at me. "With Eitaro?" I ask.

"No, Yukiko. That was only for you." Okasan smiles at me in her motherly way. This is the smile that always reassures me. "Eitaro has found a mistress in one of the teahouses in Gion. He won't be troubling you anymore."

I must have been holding my breath because I find myself breathing again.

"Eitaro was in love with you. Did you understand that? He isn't coming back, but I think it's important that you know."

Okasan sits in silence and watches me. Her eyes ask me to go deeper.

"Okasan, I understand what you are saying. All of this troubled me deeply when I first went to live with the Buddhist sisters. But in time I found a way to forgive him, and that opened the door for me to find my peace again. I understand now that Eitaro loved me, but love isn't enough. I'm not just an ornament he can wear on his arm. I have my own life and need my own life — that's what he didn't understand.

"Love isn't an ornament that you can put on and take off like a kimono on a Thursday evening. It's a powerful force that shapes two people's lives. Love isn't just about words or dreams or ideas — it demands action. That's what Eitaro didn't understand. I accept this and I forgive him, but I couldn't continue the way he wanted. I had to be free to find the shape of my own life. I need more than an unfinished dream or a distant voice.

"Kenji isn't free to shape his life with me because of the life he has chosen in the Buddhist temple, but he has loved me in a deep and steady way. It's way beyond what Eitaro could understand. Maybe other people would see this as a compromise, but it doesn't bother me now. When I needed him, he was there, even when I couldn't speak or tell him. I'll never forget how gentle he was when he walked with me by the Kamo River to the Buddhist temple. And how kind."

Okasan is smiling now. "You probably didn't know this, but he met Anjusama every Tuesday morning by the altar at the Gion Shrine to ask about you. Then, when he came here in the afternoon to teach the geishas, he always let me know about you. Every week, as steady as the birds and the sun."

"Kenji still comes on Tuesday?"

"Why would he stop?"

I look at Okasan, and I look at my bare feet on the tatami. My feet are slices of melon, birds curling over rocks. Where have they taken me now?

Okasan has eyes like Anjusama. She watches me with an amused look on her face. "Yukiko, there isn't anyone here like you. You have a different soul. Go to paint on Tuesday and you'll see. We meet with him after the midday meal in the garden."

"You?"

"Yes, why not?" Okasan's eyes still look amused. "Maybe

113

I am an old hen, but I can still learn something new."

"Do you paint?"

"Yes, but I'm only a beginner." Okasan smiles, and then she seems as if she is getting lost inside a memory. "When you first came to the geisha house as a young girl, there were many things I taught you. You were always very quick to learn. Kenji tells me that Anjusama finished your training at the Buddhist temple where you lived."

Suddenly I am laughing. I can't see myself, but I know my eyes are wild. Finished my training? Of course, a Zen priestess is not going to tell me that. She'll wait in silence until I see it myself.

Now we are both laughing. Okasan's cheeks are soft and flushed like persimmons. I think I'll paint them tonight in a wash of light and shadow.

"Kenji said that before you went to live with the Buddhist sisters, your paintings were full of dreams and beauty. They played with the shapes of your obsessions and filled themselves with the light and the laughter of the world. But the textures of the shadows were incomplete.

"That is what you needed to learn with the sisters, even if at the time you didn't know."

I am in my inner world again, following my dreams like a river, thinking about the way a painting or a poem always takes you on its own imaginative pathway and how you never know in advance where it's going to go. I am wandering in my inner world of paint. I am flinging ink against my dreams, hoboku style. Now I am painting persimmons, but the persimmon becomes a woman, and then a dream. Then a river, then my mother, then my home. A dragonfly floats out of the sun, lands on hoboku ink with the spontaneity of the accidental. Life is always a surprise.

I don't even notice what I am doing with my hands until the painting is done. Now Okasan's voice is pulling me through a texture of light and shadow until I am back in the room completely.

"Yukiko, painting is new for me, and you are a master. It's time for me to learn from you.

"While you were at the temple, many of our clients asked for you."

I look up at her, surprised. "Why? I am a wild typhoon, and the teahouse is full of pretty women."

"Yes, but not like you. We're having a party tonight for some gentlemen from Osaka. Satomi will be there with her new friend, and all of your geisha sisters will be dancing. Bring your basket of paint, and we'll see what happens after dinner. But now the sun is falling into the garden, and I need to rest for a while. I'll see you in the banquet room tonight."

I watch Okasan's feet as she walks into the garden. Something about this is nicely familiar — a backdrop for something in me that has changed. Sometimes it isn't possible to understand a change in your soul until later. You don't realize how different you are or how far you have walked until you look back. Now with the clients who come to the teahouse, I am Yukiko the artist, the wild and mysterious one.

35

THE PAINT OF
NEW BEGINNINGS

kasan was the Queen Bee at the party last night — the matriarch presiding in her court. She paints like a six-year-old, but the older gentlemen love her. I know she was a beauty when she was younger, and even close to her seventieth birthday, she hasn't lost her charm. Also, this was a good way for me to come back into the flower and willow world.

I am somewhat reluctant to return to my life as a geisha in Pontocho. I know this is the life I have chosen, but everything inside me is new, and I don't know the shape of it yet. I live in the empty space of the uncreated.

I know that I love to paint, and I don't want to feel that anyone owns me. That much is clear. Everything else is paint inside the unknown. I am a blackberry growing on a branch that is still invisible — a branch high in the mountains covered with snow. I am the paint of new beginnings — the shape of things still unformed.

I don't go out with gentlemen alone anymore, but I bring my paint and my shakuhachi flute to all of the banquets in the geisha house and to some of the parties at the teahouses down the road. The shape of my music is wild, and the men who visit the teahouses want to float inside the melodies I create. The men who are daring want to speak with me.

Rumors travel fast in the geisha community. In less than a week, everyone knows that Yukiko, the wild artist who disappeared many months ago, has come back. The men who visit the flower and willow world ask for me more than ever now. I would need two weeks inside of one to accept all the invitations that come for me to the geisha house. I let Okasan decide where I will go each night because she enjoys that so much. To me it's all the same.

I'm still exploring the shape of my emotions. Before I lived in the Buddhist temple, I was known as artistic, wild and independent. But when I look back to that time, I see how obligated I felt. The geisha society has many rules, many layers of obligation. Some of these I love the way I love ritual at the temple, but I don't want to feel obligated anymore. I want to do what I like, and not do what I don't like.

Before I lived with the Buddhist nuns, I didn't let myself feel all of my emotions. Some were unacceptable — that's what I was told — but I felt them push against my life as a geisha, even if they couldn't take a form or find a shape. I let myself feel everything now, and it's often a surprise, like a wind that comes from an unexpected direction.

I paint my emotions every morning, and this takes many forms — a row of round red lanterns, the shadings of a raku bowl, or the white powder on a maiko's face. Sometimes it's less specific — a layer of ink wash inside the wind. I haven't been finding words for these images yet. I watch them come into being and just enjoy the shape.

It almost feels like I have a new body — even though someone who isn't me couldn't see what I see reflected in the water. Maybe the new body is hidden somewhere under the skin, somewhere inside. Some of the ways I act are mysterious now, even to me, but inside of that I feel quietly confident.

I haven't gone to see Kenji yet because I want to see who I am by myself right now. Okasan tells me to listen to my heart and take my time. Every moment is new, and the new part is growing as if from a silk cocoon, from inside. It's a thread I follow day by day as it is spinning. I haven't been writing poems because I haven't found the language. Everything is still tone, music and shape.

I still paint my dreams, but my dreams are different now. I am a copper moon floating across the sky. I am the cotton of the snowflake and the glass arm of its ephemeral sculptured shape. I am the sumi-e brush strokes of a gate about to open, and I am a willow who doesn't want to break a second time.

36

LISTEN TO THE DRAGONFLIES

 month has gone by, maybe two, but now it is Tuesday morning, and I feel someone gently pulling me. This morning I painted a trellis of morning-glory vines with two dragonflies whirling into the sweet melody of a song. The dragonflies whispered, "Yukiko, go to the garden. Someone is waiting for you there."

I follow the dragonflies as they melt into ink tones and watch the shape of their wings. Dragonflies are always messengers. That's how I know the shape of my life is changing again.

Kenji has been teaching calligraphy to a small group of geishas and Kabuki actors every Tuesday afternoon. They paint in the garden, and then he reads to them from Buddhist scripture. Okasan told me about this many weeks ago, but it didn't feel right to go at that time. She understood. She knows me like a mother, and her words are wise: "You have to listen to your heart. Your heart will tell you when it's time."

121

But today I have to listen to the dragonflies. After my midday meal with Okasan, we walk together to the garden. I carry my brushes, ink, and rice paper as we walk into the afternoon sun. I breathe hibiscus and listen to the soft sound of my sandals as we walk along the stones in the garden.

When Kenji sees me, he smiles because he can see the peace in my eyes. At first I sit in silence, but I feel him penetrate me, layer by layer. He hasn't touched me in months, but there is so much love in his eyes that I open completely and let him all the way inside.

I take out my brushes and paint — it all feels like a meditation. The images are coming from a deep place inside me now. While I am painting, words fall out of my brush in calligraphic shapes. This is the first time they have come since I left the Buddhist temple, and they shape themselves into a poem:

KENJI

Since the morning the earth began
two pine trees
reaching from shadow to light
on top of the same
snow mountain.

Sometimes winding together,
sometimes growing through distances.

The sun surrounds the branches from behind.

I laugh until my voice
fills the open field with light.

A whirl of snowflakes falls toward the earth
from a distant star.

This is where I find your eyes again.
This is how I know
I am home.

37

BORN WITH THE DAWN

t first I only want to paint with Kenji. After so many months apart, this is an exquisite joy. But after many weeks go by, I want to touch him. Kenji wants this too. I think we all need to be touched when we live in a human body.

When we come together alone, it feels holy. It's also mysterious and new. It's been such a long time since Kenji and I have met this way that we've almost forgotten how to kiss each other. But it's exquisite to remember. We are two hungry mouths in moonlight, rediscovering how.

I don't regret the time I spent apart from Kenji. I needed to be away from him so that I could have my own dreams and interpret them myself. I have a pile of dreams in my basket. Paintings and poems from four different seasons. I offer these to Kenji now as my gift, as he offers me his hands, his face, and his mouth.

When Kenji first came to the geisha house, I had to teach

him everything about love, but we are equal now. I paint with the same wild effortless strokes as he does, although in a different form because I am a woman. In matters of love, Kenji is a master sculptor, and I let him shape me under his fingertips. He creates me every night.

Something about the way we love has more freedom now. This is so new that it's still a mystery. Maybe I had to be wounded to feel so much peace. Maybe I had to lose my voice to find it again.

Kenji's love goes deeper now, and I am the one who opens my skin to let him further inside. I am the mountain goddess who dies every night and is born with the dawn each morning. I am the child who flies across the sky in the morning star. I love in a white heat. Maybe the wound I had is the center of this mystery.

38

ONE LINGERING MYSTERY

There are times when life is so transparent that every emotion becomes a painting or a poem. Lately I have become obsessed with the landscape of the human body. Kenji's arms and legs have become shades of paint under my fingers. The muscles of his back are mountains in a play of light and shadow. His fingers open into brush strokes, and when I gaze into his eyes, I fall into the sky.

My art is going deeper now, into the emotions I didn't permit before. I swim in everything I feel, and the paint discovers the shape. I am the rain, the sky, and the temple fire. I am the weave of lovers and the river running through their dreams. I am the voice of the cicada under the moon, and the thunder crashing across the morning sky. Everything I see speaks to me, and every moment is new.

Some of the geishas I live with have patrons now. Chifumi lives in Hokkaido with her lover and two children, and

Oyuki lives with her daughter in the geisha house. Komami disappears with a famous Kabuki actor for long vacations in Atami. My way has always been different. I have a monk lover who visits me after midnight and disappears each morning with the dawn. I fall asleep in his arms each night, and he covers me with the petals of the moon.

In the morning my time is my own. I meditate, paint, and play my shakuhachi flute. Kenji doesn't have to sit at my table as though I were an ordinary wife — we are connected inside. In certain ways, he doesn't give me what other men can, but in other ways, he gives much more. I accept this now.

There is still one lingering mystery. I know what a blessing it is to live in a Buddhist temple, and I can't let Kenji break his vows.

39

CEREMONY
OF LOVE

I t's Tuesday afternoon, and Kenji and I are painting together in the garden. I listen to the music of the Kamo River and paint the ripple of water over stones. Kenji is painting a mountain that lifts into the clouds. He closes his eyes, then adds seven cranes circling into the wind. He gazes into my eyes and moves his brush again. In the shadings of the mountain, I can see my face.

I gaze at him again, and he has a mysterious look in his eyes, playful and wild. I want to touch him, but this is something I can't do in the open afternoon light. Still, he feels my desire, and he smiles.

I see that playful look again. "What is it, Kenji? Tell me!" I want to know what he is thinking.

"Yukiko, I want to do a ceremony with you. One of your angels flew into my dream last night, and she told me about a deep desire you have that you haven't told anyone."

"What kind of ceremony? I haven't talked to the Snow Angels since I left the Buddhist temple." I don't understand what he's talking about, but I love the music of his voice. I love the light in his eyes. I love his kindness, and I love the easy rhythm of his breathing when he holds me at night.

"A ceremony of love."

"But Kenji, how can that be? You are a Buddhist monk, and I am a geisha."

"Yukiko, both of us have lived in the Buddhist temple, and we both love ritual. We will create our own. I saw something very beautiful last night, and I want to share it with you. I want to take it out of the place where we dream and create it in our lives."

"You say I have a desire that I haven't told anyone?"

"It's something you buried so deep that even you have forgotten. But somewhere inside you know, and I'm going to take you there on Thursday night. Sometimes when people have dreams that can't find the light for many years, they turn inside themselves and hide in the shadows. Or they slip inside cracks in rocks so they don't cause you pain anymore.

"But some of these dreams are too strong and too special to be lost. They tumble into the river, and slowly, over time, the water seeps into the cracks. As the river flows, the stones tumble into geodes, and crystals grow inside. Some of them are clear, some are amethyst, some reflect the colors of the sky. Some have flecks of metal in the stone, but all of them are hidden dreams, waiting for the right time to be found and cracked and opened.

"When I hold you in my arms, I see the geodes of your hidden dreams. And when I dream with you, the crystals in the stones you paint speak to me until their voices fill the night."

I am so filled with emotion that my words are swimming.

130

They float between the river stones, far away from me. Kenji smiles and brushes his fingers over my mouth. Silently, we walk to the edge of the garden.

Under the branches of the willow tree, I play my shakuhachi flute. Kenji listens — the music says everything. When the sun falls into the plum trees, he kisses the top of my head and says, "I'll come to see you on Thursday. When the moon is full above the trees, meet me at the bath house."

40

HOUSE OF
DREAMS

 t's Thursday night, and the moon is floating full above the branches of the persimmon trees. The night air of Kyoto is still humid with late summer heat. Earlier in the evening I was playing my flute at a birthday celebration for one of Okasan's oldest clients and performing traditional dances with two of my geisha sisters. But now my time is my own.

I walk over the stones to the bath house in a new kimono. I wanted to wear something for Kenji that is worthy of this ceremony. I know that my open heart is enough, but I am a woman too, and a geisha. This is one of my ways. My hair is full of flowers, and I shiver with anticipation. At the same time I am as calm as the moonlight falling on my hands.

I open the door to the bath house, and the room is lit by candles. Kenji has prepared the room for me. He is sitting on the tatami mat in full lotus with his eyes closed. Slowly, he opens his eyes, bows to me, and says,

"Welcome to the House of Dreams."

A flood of memories comes back. I remember the first time I loved him here and the way I bathed him with my hands. My heart is as full as the moon, as open as a thousand-petaled lotus. I remember the way he shivered when I touched him, even though the room was filled with heat and steaming water. Now we are in this room again, and his hands are pulling me into the future.

Kenji reaches for my face, and his lips brush my mouth. Slowly, he opens the rose petals of my kimono and lifts it off my shoulders.

"I love your eyes, your face, your heart, your poetry, your music, and your body is the most beautiful sculpture in the world. I remember when I first saw you and recognized the hidden wisdom in your eyes. I remember when I first loved you and felt all that fire. You are my wild earth goddess. My eyes and my heart adore you."

He gazes at me with his eyes full of love. Then he lifts his robe over his shoulders and leads me to the bath. We walk hand in hand down the blue tile steps, and now we are shoulder high in steaming water. One by one, Kenji lifts out my hairpins. Free of its sculptured form, my hair slides over my shoulders into a dark waterfall. Gardenias float around us as he follows my hair with his hands.

Slowly we bathe each other — so much pleasure in my body and my hands. I watch his face illumined by candles — another exquisite joy. I breathe the humid scent of gardenias and float inside the strong support of his hands. I think about making love to him underwater, but that can wait for another time.

For a few moments I am lost in time until Kenji lifts me out of the water. The bath house glows in a peach petal fire as we dry each other slowly. This is another joy. I trace the shape of his muscles in slow circles with my fingertips as he memorizes every curve of my body one more time.

Now he folds a scarf of yellow silk over my eyes and takes my hand. He leads me over the stone path to my room at the edge of the garden. I feel the shape of the stones with my feet.

When I open my eyes, I am surrounded by candles in the shape of a lotus. Kenji and I sit on silk pillows facing each other in the center of the light. The amber light is like a cocoon. In the center of the light, Kenji's eyes melt me. Then he continues.

"Now inside the fire, we are in a sacred place." He reaches for me and pulls me into his being. At the same time I offer myself as a gift. I feel him enter me without touching. At the same time I see him open to let my feminine light inside.

We sit in silence that way, and then he reaches for seven tiny ceramic bowls and places them in a circle between us. The bowls are filled with scented oils: jasmine, lotus, hibiscus, rose, geranium, peach petals, and wisteria.

He takes the first bowl in his hand and whispers, "Now I anoint you with sacred oil." He draws a circle of jasmine at the top of my head with his finger. "I'm sealing my love inside your body."

He spirals lotus oil around the center of my forehead. Then he anoints my throat with hibiscus, my heart with rose, my solar plexus with geranium, my womb with peach petals, and the base of my spine with wisteria. His hands are full of light. Each time his fingers trace a spiral, I feel his light surround me and flow inside.

Now it is my turn. I pick up the first bowl of oil with the hands of a priestess, steady my voice, and speak: "Now I anoint you with sacred oil." Kenji bows to me and I start with jasmine oil at the top of his head, and follow with lotus, hibiscus, rose, geranium, peach petals, and wisteria as I circle the scent of my love into his body. I know this body so well that it almost feels like mine.

He gazes into my eyes before he continues. These are the eyes I have come to love so well. Then he begins to speak.

"I promise to love and honor the lotus goddess in your heart, and to adore the divine woman in your body."

I echo his words as I tell him, "I promise to love and honor the lotus god in you, and to adore the divine man in your body."

As the candles burn around us, we continue our vows. He speaks and I answer.

"I promise to hold you in my arms when you fall asleep each night."

"And I promise to paint your face with my fingertips every morning."

"I promise to walk with you on your path to spiritual freedom."

"And I promise to fly with you between the stars."

"I promise to love you beyond time."

"And if the world falls apart, I will be your light in the uncreated darkness."

Suddenly, I am everywhere in time. The candles float around us like stars as we melt into each other. We are lost in the middle of a wild forest with silver pebbles on the path, but the stars take us home.

I am the full moon as I swim in your love. I am the tides that fill you with my salty sweetness. Tumbling underwater I am sand, I am foam. And everywhere you touch me, I send the ripples back.

41

PIECES OF
THE FUTURE

s the months go by, this is my life — half of it under teahouse lanterns, half of it in secret. I continue my life as an artist and a geisha, but Kenji comes to see me every night. He is the wild bear in the mountain story — the bear who disappears every morning, the bear who is invisible even at night until the princess lights a candle. Every night he becomes human under her hands.

We are sumi-e artists who sleep in a wash of feathers, until the feathers melt like flames of a candle with the dawn. I paint him every morning with my fingertips, and then he disappears. But I know that when the stars scatter their sparks across the sky, he'll be back.

I often think about our vows. I promise to love you beyond time. Something about this makes me shiver. Maybe these words can change time. Or maybe they are a message to the angels that guide us in between. Since the night of our ceremony in the bath house, the Snow Angels have come closer. Often they speak to me in my dreams. It's almost as if they're preparing me for something, but what, I don't know.

My dreams are different now. They go forward and backward in time. Each night is full of paint and messages. Sometimes the messages come in a language I haven't heard in this body, but something inside me knows what they mean. Sometimes I find myself crawling in the dark towards a flicker of light. It's a mystery covered by a cocoon while meteor showers explode over my shoulders.

Sometimes I can see pieces of the future. I'm free falling from the air. Floating in the dark with ribbons of silk drifting around my ankles. Banded bees are trying to tell me stories, but all I hear is a buzzing in my ears.

Kenji and I are dancing barefoot after midnight. We are covered with oil inside a steam of jasmine flowers. I run my fingers over the hills and valleys of his body before the shakuhachi music stops. We might be in Kyoto or Nagasaki, but the walls are now a blur. My heart is shaking, or maybe it is the walls. The sake, still warm from the heat of his hands, is spilling across the table as he paints on my back with ink-covered fingers.

A tunnel is streaming with silk as I crawl in the semi-dark. The bees are humming softly on the other side of the wall. The tone is silk, translucent, and floating. It's a new kind of music that I refused to listen to before. The bees say the erotic is in the shadows, and nobody can love without the wound. They tell me we all need to be pierced to know the mystery.

42

THE MUSIC WEAVES
THROUGH TIME

his morning I am painting time under a trellis of morning glory vines. The flowers weave in and out of the light, like my dreams. The river of my life has been calm and sweet as the first light of the morning. The place where it goes deep and wild is inside — in my dreams and in my art.

The men who visit the geisha house ask me if I am carrying a secret. I am, but I don't say anything. When they ask me what my secret might be, I answer with a smile or a song on the shakuhachi flute. The music weaves through time, and there's nothing I need to tell them.

Since the year turned, I've been studying pottery with a raku master. I love forming clay with my hands. It's like a massage, but with a different kind of body. A body from the Earth. I like the idea of a goddess with clay feet, eyes like the center of stars, the moon in her belly, and vines growing out of her mouth. As I paint the vines, they become pregnant with blossoms.

Sometimes I think about having a child, but the Birth Angels always say, "No, not this time." They tell me to give birth with paint or clay instead. They say, "You have been chosen for a different kind of art."

Kenji and I have been reading out loud from Tibetan Buddhist scripture. The monks in the temple where he lives have been translating these books into Japanese. I love hearing sacred words in Kenji's voice. His voice is so musical, so warm. The books describe all of the stages of meditation, layers of light, and the journey the soul takes after the body returns to clay.

I've been painting the visions I see from these words in glazes on a series of clay pots. I love the way the glazes transform and burn inside the fire. A soul journey in clay right in front of my eyes. After the fire, the glaze is textured and translucent. The colors sing.

Since Kenji still teaches the geishas each Tuesday afternoon, the Roshi gave him a book about ecstatic sexual union as a path of spiritual transformation. I know I'm looking at this through the eyes of a geisha, but I see mischief in that man. Maybe he knows more than Kenji wants to believe. Kenji reads me a new page of translation every night. We practice these techniques for hours until we are both completely wild. Another path of transformation through fire. Another kind of singing.

Sometimes I worry that the Roshi will discover Kenji's night journeys. Kenji doesn't worry about this at all. He loves both of his lives, and they both feel right to him. At the center of everything, he feels a deep tranquility. Even when he is totally wild.

The only thing that confuses me now is the dreams where the Birth Angels come and speak to me. They speak to me in a different language. At night I understand, but I can't remember the translation in the morning. Something is missing — a shape I can't paint in the middle of the forest, a dragonfly without wings, a fish made of shadow in the middle of a koi pond.

Kenji says I should try to remember the sounds, even if I can't pull the meaning through the veil.

43

THE
INTRUDER

Last night an intruder walked into my room while we were sleeping. This could be dangerous. If the intruder was a thief, there is nothing except ink paintings, poems, raku bowls, and chrysanthemums. He can help himself. But what if the intruder was the Roshi? Kenji's robes and sandals were on the floor, latticed by strips of moonlight from the slatted window.

I cannot go to the temple where he lives. Geishas are not permitted to walk inside those walls, so I have to wait. The monks are in silence now, and I won't see Kenji until Thursday.

Kenji always laughs when I am worried. When I finally speak to him, he says the intruder was probably a sad and lonely man who needed to see two people in love. He says the way we were curved around each other must have healed him. It must have been something he needed to see, or he wouldn't have been there. He says the way his hand was lightly touching my hip must have brought our visitor a quiet joy. It was a vision to shake a part of him that was sleeping. He says it is an honor to be part of this transformation.

His words are amber threads of honey, the filaments of a song. They soothe my emotions, but my intuition is still ringing like a temple bell. Something is wrong. I don't know the shape of it, but a shadow is hovering over the room. His dark fingers weave shadows on the shoji screen. At night I am afraid to dream, but Kenji says he will hold me until the dawn to take my fear away. He promises me that this night will be peaceful.

Long after midnight Kenji holds me in his arms — there is so much strength and peace there. I feel his arms comfort me as I fall asleep.

I know that I am sleeping, but my eyes are wide open in a different place. I am in the Buddhist temple, and the Roshi hits the gong. He is chanting the prayers for Megumi. White deer run through the windows, and the temple is filled with light.

The Snow Angels come and lead me to a ladder. My bare feet climb the feathers into the sky. The feathers are blue. I sing as I tumble through clouds scented with gardenias.

Megumi waits for me at the top of the ladder. A gardenia opens in each of her hands as she pulls me into the light. She says, "I will meet you here in seven days." Then she disappears.

44

PAINTING
THUNDERSTORMS

n the morning I forget about the dream. The sun is scraping the trees, and Kenji is already gone. But later, when I am walking outside in a field of goats, the images from the other world come back. I remember everything from last night and even more.

I am walking in a field of goats in another country a long time ago, but it also feels like now. A woman with dark eyes, tan skin, and black curly hair walks out from the middle of the goats. She has bare feet with silver ankle bracelets and holds a baby goat in her arms — a goat that was born this morning.

She walks up to me. Her eyes are familiar, full of sunlight. Maybe she knows more than I do right now. "What is your name?" I ask, and she says, "Ayellet. In your language this means 'Morning Star' or 'Deer of the Dawn.'" She takes my hands and kisses me softly on the mouth. Then she sings until she disappears.

Now I am looking through a waterfall. I realize the goats are a memory, and the woman with wild dark hair is me. But it's me in another place and time.

I spin into a pirouette, and Ayellet walks through the water. She is milking one of the goats at the edge of a long, green pasture. This is mysterious to me — I have never seen this in Japan — but I watch her. Then she gives me milk to drink out of her hands.

As I am drinking, her face dissolves, and now we are both earlier in time. There are pyramids all around and a blue river in the distance. A woman with a gold band across her fore-head walks out of a pyramid. She has my eyes, but a different face. "What is your name?" I ask, and she says, "Isis. I am a priestess in the temple." She leads me into the pyramid and puts an amethyst in my hand. For a long time we gaze into each other's eyes. Then she walks back into the river.

Now we are in the Egyptian Isis temple. My ankles are wild, dancing with ribbons of tiny silver bells. The temple is round inside a circle of crystals. Isis and I are swirling inside the rhythm of the bells. The silver becomes music around our feet; the drumbeat comes from behind. Isis lifts the veil from her eyes and hands me a tambourine. I am spinning, ecstatic, wild, as the silver music flies to the edges of what I can see. Then the edges disappear.

I am back in Japan again, in the garden of the temple at Oshidoridera. Everything I hear and see is washing into me like paint, and I am the rice paper scroll for the ink. The blossoms of cherry trees are soaking into me in layers; the painting that I am changes every day. Every stone on the road sings to me. There is a message from every leaf on every tree. Every wind changes the texture of my skin into the wild geometry of longing.

Every thought that I've ever had is breathing. I don't

know if I am here or in another world. I don't know if it is day or night or a dream.

A tambourine is spinning, and now I am looking at my life five years ago. I think about everything I can't control, and my shoulders tighten. I feel the thin thread of pain that sometimes troubles me in my sleep. Maybe if I can find a way to tie Kenji to my bed, the hollow below my shoulder blade won't hurt me in the morning. But I don't want Kenji that way. I want him to come by himself.

I am walking through a thunderstorm. The rain soaks my kimono. At the same time I know that every step is right. They just aren't the steps that I would choose if I were writing the scroll. This troubles me, but there's nothing to do except keep walking.

At the edge of the garden, I walk through a waterfall, and now I am back in the Buddhist temple. I remember that I don't think that way anymore. Now I am cooking soup with the Buddhist nuns, and I am filled with a quiet peace. I stir the soup until it becomes a river.

I take out my rice paper and ink. I am learning a new technique from one of the sumi-e masters in the temple. It's called tarashikomi — you brush water across the paper and layer the ink in a wash. Then the layers blend and create a shape you couldn't have planned or predicted. It's ink out of control, but taking the right shape by itself. Yes, this is the way to paint. This is my life.

The late afternoon light is scraping my elbows like a dream. I won't see Kenji again until next Thursday. I have to leave him a message, but what can it be? If I get my brushes, I will find the words inside the paint.

I close my eyes and brush the water across the page. Then the ink, one layer after another. Forget about control. I am painting thunderstorms. Dawn is here again and Kenji is gone.

I can't see Isis anymore, but I can feel her in the shadows. I feel her in the paint and hear her whisper, "Kenji will get the message. Tonight, he will see your painting when he dreams."

45

A LAYER
OF SILK

know that Kenji had an important dream last night — I can feel it in my body — but I won't see him until Thursday late at night. Time is sticking together at the edges like crystals of snow and moving slowly. At night my vision is clear, but during the day, snow covers everything.

When I wake up in the morning, I am at the edge of two different worlds, feeling my way with my hands at the border. At first I can walk through both of them, but as the light gets stronger, the first world disappears. I walk through the daylight world, forgetting everything. It's a world where I can only paint to remember.

It's even hard to remember if Kenji came into my dreams between the shadows. I can only tell from the scent of jasmine around my feet if I catch it before it disappears. Or from the last edges of a candle burning. The candle speaks to me: "The Voice of the Fire tells the Truth. Walk into her fingers. The flames won't burn your hair this time."

My geisha sisters say I have disappeared into another world, even though I walk with them in the morning. How can I tell them? How could they understand? I don't even understand.

I am preparing tea for Okasan, but I am walking between a world of light and shadow. My thoughts flow in a wash of sumi-e ink tones. Eros always creates impossible longings. I brush them into the shape of a flying dragon, a serpent with wings. I paint Kenji's face in the cliffs on the side of a mountain. Now I am drying his feet with my hair.

"Where are you, Yukiko?" Okasan is reaching for her tea from a tray of yamato-e irises. Her voice almost pulls me back.

"Mama, I don't know. I am walking on a road that I have never seen before."

"Where is Kenji?"

"He is in silence. He will be with the monks for another three days."

Okasan watches my face as a cloud covers the sun. A flock of blackbirds swarm into a cherry tree in the garden. Their voices are a harem of tambourines. A wind is blowing west from the mountains as birds fly through the branches.

"Mama, something happens at night when I sleep, but I forget in the morning. Whatever it is feels more real than what I see during the day, but after the dawn light reaches into the morning, I can't remember. My eyes are full of snow."

"Maybe you're dreaming about the shape of the future, but the angels always cover that with a layer of silk. The future has to be a mystery."

"But I want to know."

"You and everyone, Yukiko." Okasan takes another sip of tea and speaks again. "Maybe you are preparing for another birth."

"Is someone pregnant?"

"That's not what I'm talking about. I just want you to remember what you learned when you helped your sister with her first child. It will help you now."

The trees are filling up with birds, every bird singing a different song, and I follow the weave of their melodies. Suddenly I am smiling again. I open the window and lean out with my flute. A hummingbird hovers around my hand, and I answer with a melody.

Okasan watches smiling, and I feel like myself again. At least for a few minutes now.

"Okasan, you are the perfect midwife for an artist."

"And you are the perfect artist. I never know what you'll do next."

"Well it's good that one of us has her feet in her sandals. Whatever I need to know is exactly what I forget."

"Yukiko, don't worry about it. You always feel this way when your life is going through a transition. Just enjoy the mystery."

"Okasan, how do you know these things?"

"Yukiko, you have only lived twenty-seven years. I am seventy-two. I've seen many things, many seasons, many faces, and time is a wise teacher. I've raised two daughters and a house full of geisha women. Each one with her moods, her joys, and her bleeding. It makes you patient."

I watch Okasan's hands around the teacup. These hands are so precious to me. I watch her face, round as the full moon. I can't imagine my life without this face. I want to paint her face. I want to fill her life with music.

I hear the tambourine of the birds again. The sky changes shape until the clouds are goats running through a wide blue gorge. My face fills with light, and suddenly everything becomes silver.

46

BRIDGE BETWEEN
NIGHT AND MORNING

ometimes I think the moon is a silver bowl with God in the middle and flying fish swimming all around. Maybe that's the truth about what some people call falling stars. They actually aren't falling — they're flying. Maybe they'd look like fish swimming through the sky if you could see them from the moon. Or from the back of one of the other fish.

I know, I dreamed about one of these fish last night and took a ride on a wide arc through the sky. The fish are what some of the Buddhists call bodhisattvas — saints who have received a spiritual illumination but come back here to help other people see it too. These people don't have to be born, but they come back out of compassion for the rest of us, lit up from inside. They become teachers or quiet saints who live around the corner and never claim to be different from anyone else. The only difference is that inside, they know something that the rest of us are trying to find. But in between lives, when they are out of their bodies, they fly around the sky inside of stars. Even people who don't know this make wishes when they see them burning their path of fire through the sky.

I know that it is possible to speak to God face to face, but how? Everyone has to find her own way. Maybe at night when I am flying between the stars, I can find a bridge to cross over and meet him on the other side. Or maybe build my own bridge on a path of sculpted wood over a koi pond. I want to build my bridge out of wood I find in the forest or on a mountain. I want the bridge to twist and bend in unexpected directions, the way life does. That feels realistic to me. And I want to plant flowers in unexpected places. Jasmine, lilies and hibiscus.

What I like best about flowers is their unexpected beauty. A gentle surprise, like the strong arms of a lover. I always forget in between. My memory for touch or beauty can keep me in another world for three days. Like the scent of a yellow rose. But then the vision fades, and I need to be reminded again.

Loving Kenji is like walking across a bridge made of sand. Or flying stars. I walk across his back, but it has become a constellation of asteroids, lost in the Milky Way, or stones in a Japanese rock garden. We swim all night and then he disappears. In the morning I am naked, covered with sand.

Anyhow, here is my plan for meeting God. I build my bridge of twigs and logs over the koi pond, but the pond gets bigger and bigger every night. I gather wood for the bridge from different places in time — the forest, the mountains, the edge of the river, my memories, and my dreams. The bridge is a bird's nest, but in a different shape. I put it together like a nightingale gathering twigs and string and bits of silver. I carry the pieces through time with my mouth, and after midnight I shape the pieces into a web of living sculpture. But still, it's a spell created out of mud. It's a bird's nest, and it exists out of time.

The twigs are artifacts of time, but I can walk across them. I am a sculptor, and everything I create with my hands becomes real. I am a nightingale, and this is the way I create the shape of my world.

I gather the moonlight in a silver bowl and pour it over my hair. I am a room full of light and shadows. I am a night with the breeze blowing wisteria and hibiscus through the open window. I am a night traveler on a bridge I built with my hands. I carry my brushes and rice paper as I walk, and I leave the sumi-e shapes of my journey everywhere the bridge unexpectedly turns.

Now I am walking across the bridge I have built, which is also the bridge between night and morning. I'm dancing, wild with moonlight in my hair. My skin is breathing hibiscus. Suddenly, there is an earthquake. This happens in Japan. The bridge completely dissolves, becomes sand, becomes waves, and I meet God underwater.

47

I Am the Moon,
He Is the Sun

It's Tuesday evening — not the usual time. Kenji waits until the moon is floating above the branches of the plum trees over the lily pond. Then he comes to my door and tells me a dream.

"It was four o'clock in the morning. I was sitting by a waterfall in a deep state of meditation. My body was perfectly still and suspended inside the water — I was a monk and a rainbow at the same time. I was exactly who I am and also everywhere.

"Ten monks in robes the color of snow walked out of a mountain. The monks sat down in a circle around me and waited until I opened my eyes. Then they waited longer and looked at me. I felt very old and at the same time like a child.

"Finally one of the monks spoke to me. He said, 'You have gone to the limit of what you can learn in this robe, so I want you to take it off.' He stood in front of me with his two hands open, waiting. I slowly untied the rope around

157

my waist. Then I lifted my monk's robe over my head and put it in his hands.

"I stood before him naked, and he continued. 'There's something you need to know before you leave this planet, and the way to learn is when you are naked as a child. The time is next Tuesday.'

"That was all he said. There was a long silence where our eyes burned into each other. Then he stepped back into the circle. The monks circled around me, and one by one, they put their hands on my head to bless and release me. Then they let me go."

Kenji's eyes burn into Yukiko now. Then his words find a new place inside her: "It's Tuesday, and it's time."

Kenji unties the rope to his robe. Like the ceremony of tea, he is mindful of every gesture. With complete attention he folds his robe and offers it to Yukiko. She is the yellow rose that has just fully bloomed this morning. She is the altar.

Silently, he follows her to the bath house. So much joy in the walking. There is a poem in her bare ankles dancing over the stones. He watches them disappear and then appear again below the hem of her red kimono.

Yukiko's joy is floating out of her mouth. Her mouth is filled with hummingbirds flying in and out of the petals of white chrysanthemums. The birds fly out of her mouth in the music of a song. As she sings it, the song changes her voice.

She opens the door of the bath house and turns to face the man she adores. They stand before each other but can't find any words. It's all in the eyes. She starts to unwrap the obi from around her kimono, but he stops her hand.

He speaks softly. "I have to look at you first. Whenever I have been in this room before, there has always been a door between us — a sacred place I was not allowed to enter." He takes her face in his hands. "Now I want to look at your face with all the petals open."

Slowly he unwraps her obi, then lifts her kimono from her shoulders. One layer of silk gone to reveal the next. He kisses her shoulders, then her neck, then her eyes. "Our love has no barriers now. No doors, only windows."

He asks permission with his eyes, and her eyes answer. As he penetrates, she feels his light enter, first her body, then deeper. Now he is inside her, and her edges melt. She is swimming inside a sky of falling stars. Running through a forest of wild bears.

Yukiko and Kenji swim in each other for hours, while the moon rises higher and higher in the sky. The air is humid, full of the scent of gardenias. They are everywhere in time. They are loving each other inside the steam of the bath house in Pontocho. They are walking the long row of stone lanterns to the Sengen-Jinja Shrine at Fuji Yoshida. Kenji's voice is calling down the falling stars as they burn their path of fire across the sky. At the same time, his voice is the call to prayer, drifting out of the tower of the mosque and floating through the late afternoon. Yukiko's back is the arch of the minaret that follows the path of the horizon.

When you open yourself completely to another human being, you enter a world beyond space and time — beyond the male and female boundaries of the human body. You're making love, but you're wild inside the forest, moving towards the other, but at the same time moving inward through your own layers of body and consciousness. The outer layer is your physical body. As you go deeper, the layers become less and less physical, less and less of a costume.

The body is what makes you a man or a woman and determines what the experience will be, but as you move in, deeper and deeper in the forest, as you move through physical, sexual, heart and soul, the inner sexuality, which contains both male and female, comes through. At a certain point, there is a choice. My male/female essence meets you. Your female/male essence meets me. The inner man and woman are facing each other deep inside.

As a woman, my heart is open. My legs are wide and wrapped around you, and I feel the penetration. But we are so far inside each other that I feel your male essence as strongly as I feel my own. At that moment my sexuality becomes more direct and penetrating. Like dancing, you pick it up with a look in the eye.

You're in the wild forest, and it's easy. The forest is filled with bears and blossoms of rhododendron trees. The trees are filled with songbirds just after sunrise, and the melodies weave together into a larger song. We love each other completely, without hesitation. We're separate, joined, and at the center of all possibilities. This is the point of creation where long ago we were formed as human beings.

At that point you can choose. Let my inner woman fill you. Let your inner man fill me. I am still inside my body, but you are in me even deeper. Reach for me and pull me into your being. Pour yourself into my eyes. On the deepest altar of my heart, my emotions, and my inner light, I offer myself as a gift. To you completely. I just give it, and everything changes inside. I slide into you, you slide into me, ripples emerge where the waters meet inside.

Time has dissolved, and we have entered a state of intense communion. I'm so far inside you that I don't even remember where I am. I remember making love to you in different bodies, different lives. Sometimes as a man, sometimes as a woman. Sometimes with my body. Sometimes only with my eyes.

I don't know where I stop and where you begin. We have become each other completely. Time has dissolved until we are somewhere else in time, another place where I have become a monk, and you are a woman.

When I look with my inner eyes, I see Kenji as a woman now. She has a different face with eyes I almost remember. She has a different name, and I am washing her feet. I wrap her feet with silver anklets, and now I hear the silver music of her steps before we take our wedding vows.

Suddenly, Kenji sees me as a man. I am wearing an ochre robe on top of a high mountain in Tibet, and Kenji's hands are blessing me. He rests them lightly on my head like a crown. As I take my monk's vows, I feel the light pour into me through his fingers.

Now he is a woman again, and this is the woman that I am in my body. I feel myself enter him as he enters me — simultaneously.

I am a woman again, but now I can feel the mastery of each stroke as he swims inside me. I feel the glide and the power of every thrust from the inside of his body. I feel the muscled power of this man like an oak tree that has seen everything in the forest for a hundred years. I feel the power of his touch wake me up where I was sleeping under the thorns. Where I was sleeping under a lake after I forgot how to sing.

I am a tiny child, and my eyes are open for the first time in this body. I fill myself with the light that pours through his eyes and his hands. In his touch the power of the whole earth enters me. I have never been more awake, as the birds of a new morning fill the trees and sing through my fingers. My voice is new again, and a song is leaving my throat in syllables I have never sung before.

I am the moon, he is the sun, and we are swimming in each other's light. We are dragonflies, mating in circles above the koi pond. We are all of the planets orbiting in space. I am here, in my body, in his body, and everywhere at the same time.

Time has become linear and simultaneous. Every edge is an open window. I can't locate myself, unless I am everywhere.

Suddenly the earth is shaking. The lacquer vase rolls on the floor, scattering the chrysanthemums, and the shoji screen crashes into the wall. The shaking gets more intense and it doesn't stop. Somehow it doesn't matter. We gaze into each other's eyes as he holds me in his arms. As I rock in my sweet monk's arms, I hear the grinding of boulders in the distance. The last thing I remember is the weight of the teahouse falling on my head.

48

CANDLES AND GARDENIAS

I t's one hundred and fifty years later. I live across the Great Ocean to the east. I slid down the Earth Tunnel to the continent the copper-skinned people who migrated here from Asia call Turtle Island, and I speak English now instead of Japanese. I was born into a Jewish/Egyptian bloodline, the third child after two brothers. Megumi is my sister, but she has a different name.

My family is artistic, which is a delight to me. Our house is full of books, sculpture and music. As we grow my parents give us lessons in painting, piano and ballet, along with the freedom to be ourselves.

In the sacred texts, they say your physical form is the composite of every place you have been. As I grow to be a woman, I have wild Yemenite hair, Russian dancer eyes, pale skin, an Egyptian face, and a Japanese body.

Kenji was born just above the northern border in a city

by a lake. He is Japanese but his family gave him an English name. They crossed the ocean after the Second World War because they wanted their third child to be part of a new country.

I am a dancer, which is how I meet him again. My dance troupe is on tour in the city where he lives. Something about the way I move on stage attracts his attention. Something about my legs, my eyes, and my body. He tells me later that watching me from a distance felt like a memory or a dream. It was something deeper than what he saw with his eyes — and every cell in his body was pulled to me.

He finds his way backstage somehow through a maze of stairs and tunnels and waits for me with a blood red rose. Where the rose came from is something I still don't know, but I invite him to the reception. I don't remember him at first, but as soon as we start to talk, it is immediately deep. I know much more about him than I possibly could know about a stranger holding a rose. The only thing that confuses me is how I know these things. This kind of conversation is unusual for me. I'm the kind of person who feels life through my body, and mostly I love to dance.

But something about this man pulls me in a way that I haven't been touched or understood before. The words that come out of his mouth are like music, and they turn me inside out. It's early summer with a hot wind full of flowers blowing up from the south. He asks me to stay with him for the rest of the summer, and I say yes. I'm reckless and I do things like that.

Two weeks later, we take a bath together. He fills the room with candles and gardenias. As I slide into the steam next to him, cup water over his shoulders, and explore the shape of the muscles on the landscape of his body, the tiles turn blue and the memories come back.

GLOSSARY

BODHISATTVA: A saint who has received a spiritual illumination but out of compassion for humanity, agrees to be born over and over again until everyone is enlightened.

DEVA: Sanskrit for an aspect of God.

FUROSHIKI: A square piece of cloth used to tie and carry things. Usually it has a colorful pattern.

GEI: Art.

GEISHA: Literally, "artist."

GION: One of the geisha districts in Kyoto.

HOBOKU: A style of flung ink in sumi-e painting.

KABOCHA: A type of Japanese squash.

KABUKI: Traditional Japanese theatre. There is a lot of interaction between the Kabuki and geisha communities. Sometimes geishas marry Kabuki actors.

KAMO RIVER: The river that runs through Kyoto.

KANNON: The Buddhist Goddess of Compassion. In China, she is called Quan Yin.

KOI POND: An ornamental pond stocked with carp in a Japanese garden.

KOTO: Thirteen-stringed rectangular harp.

MAIKO: A young, apprentice geisha.

MISO: Fermented soy bean paste.

NADESHIKO: Carnation-like flower.

OBI: Wide sash for a kimono.

OKASAN: Mother of a geisha house.

ORIGAMI: The art of Japanese paper folding.

OSHIDORIDERA: The older name of Ryoanji Temple in Kyoto. It means, "Temple of Mandarin Ducks."

PONTOCHO: One of the geisha districts in Kyoto.

RAKU: A style of pottery where the glaze goes directly into the fire.

ROSHI: A Zen master.

SHAKUHACHI: A bamboo flute.

SHAMISEN: Traditional stringed instrument played by geishas.

SHIATSU: A Japanese system of healing massage, acupressure.

SHOJI SCREEN: A white paper screen with cross beams of wood.

SUMI-E: Japanese ink painting.

SUTRAS: Verses of Buddhist scripture.

TAO: Literally, "the Way." The source and guiding principle of all reality, according to the Taoist religion.

TARASHIKOMI: A sumi-e technique of layering ink washes.

TATAMI: A thick mat of woven straw.

YAMATO-E: A style of Japanese painting that uses color instead of ink.

ZEN BUDDHISM: The style of Buddhism that developed in Japan.

ABOUT THE AUTHOR

Diane Frank is an award winning poet. Her friends describe her as a harem of seven women in one very small body. She has mentored hundreds of writers at San Francisco State University, City College of San Francisco, The University of Vermont, and the Professional Writing Program at MIU in Iowa. Currently, she divides her time between San Francisco, California — where she dances, plays cello, and creates her life as an art form — and Fairfield, Iowa, where she directs Poets at 8:00 and teaches writing workshops. She is also a documentary scriptwriter with expertise in eastern and sacred art. *Blackberries in the Dream House*, her first novel, has been nominated for the Pulitzer Prize.

OTHER BOOKS
BY DIANE FRANK

The Winter Life of Shooting Stars
(Blue Light Press, Fairfield, Iowa, 1999).

The All Night Yemenite Café
(Dark River Press: Davenport, Iowa, 1993).

Rhododendron Shedding Its Skin
(Blue Light Press: San Francisco, California, 1988).

Isis: Poems by Diane Frank
(Project Press: Los Angeles, California, 1982).

ANTHOLOGY PUBLICATIONS

The Book of Eros: Arts and Letters from Yellow Silk
(Harmony Books: New York, 1995).

Voices on the Landscape: Contemporary Iowa Poets
(Loess Hills Press: Iowa, 1996).

Eclipsed Moon Coins: Twenty-Six Visionary Poets
(Blue Light Press, Fairfield, Iowa, 1997).

Diane Frank
c/o 1st World Library
PO Box 2211
Fairfield, Iowa 52556
GeishaPoet@aol.com

Printed in the United States
31874LVS00001B/73-99